DIALOGUE WITH A DEMON

"Deliverer, Deliverer, Deliverer," mocked the cloud, "my pet Dilvish, little creature of hooks and chains. Do you not know your master? Is your memory so short?" and the cloud collapsed upon itself and coalesced into a bird-headed creature with the hindquarters of a lion and two serpents growing up from its shoulders, curling and engendering about its high crest of flaming quills.

"Cal-Den!"

"Aye, your old tormentor, Elf-man. I have missed you, for few depart my care. It is time you returned."

"This time," Dilvish said, "I am not chained and unarmed, and we meet in my world." He cut forward with his blade.

ROGER ZELAZNY
DILVISH, THE DAMNED

A Del Rey Book

BALLANTINE BOOKS • NEW YORK

For Joe Sanders

A Del Rey Book
Published by Ballantine Books

Library of Congress Catalog Card Number: 82-90441

ISBN 0-345-30625-2

Manufactured in the United States of America

First Edition: November 1982

Cover art by Michael Herring

CONTENTS

ACKNOWLEDGMENTS

PASSAGE
TO DILFAR

WHEN Dilvish the Damned came down from Portaroy they tried to stop him at Qaran, and again at Tugado, then again at Maestar, Mycar, and Bildesh. Five horsemen had waited for him along the route to Dilfar; and when one flagged, a new rider with a fresh horse would replace him. But none could keep the pace of Black, the horse out of steel, for whom it was said the Colonel of the East had bartered a part of his soul.

A day and a night had he ridden, to outpace the advancing armies of Lylish, Colonel of the West, for his own men lay stiff and clotted on the rolling fields of Portaroy.

When Dilvish had seen that he was the last man standing in the place of slaughter, he had called Black to his side, hauled himself into the saddle that was a part of him, and cried for an escape. Black's gleaming hooves had borne him through a line of pikemen, their staffs turned aside like wheat, and ringing, as their metal tips touched against his midnight hide.

"To Dilfar!" he had cried, and Black turned at a right angle in his course and carried him up the face of a cliff where only goats can go.

When Dilvish came by Qaran, Black turned his head and said to him: "Great Colonel of the East,

1

they have mined the air and the air beneath the air with the stars of death."

"Can you get by them?" asked Dilvish.

"If we go by way of the posting road," said Black, "I may be able to."

"Then let us make haste to try it."

The tiny silver eyes, which looked out from the space beneath space and contained the hellspecks of starstuff, blinked and shimmered ahead.

They turned off the road.

It was on the posting road that the first rider emerged from behind a boulder and called upon Dilvish to halt. His horse was a huge bay without trappings.

"Draw rein, Colonel of the East," he had said. "Thy men are slaughtered. The road ahead is seeded with death and flanked by the men of Lylish—"

But Dilvish had swept past him without making answer, and the man put his spurs to the bay and followed.

He paced him all that morning, up the road to Tugado, until the bay, who was all alather, stumbled and hurled the man to the rocks.

At Tugado Dilvish found his way blocked by the rider of the blood-red stallion, who fired at him a bolt from a crossbow.

Black reared high into the air, and the bolt glanced off his chest. His nostrils grew, with a sound like the cry of a great bird coming forth from them. The blood-red stallion leapt from the roadway then and into the field.

Black plunged ahead, and the other rider turned his horse and followed.

Till the sun reached the top of the sky did he give chase, and then the red horse collapsed in a heap of heavy breathing. Dilvish rode on.

At Maestar the way was blocked at the Pass of Reshth.

A wall of logs filled the narrow trail to twice the height of a man.

"Over," said Dilvish, and Black arced into the air

like a dark rainbow, going up and across the fortification.

Just ahead, at the ending of the pass, the rider of the white mare waited.

Black cried out once more, but the mare stood steady.

The light reflected from the mirrors of his steel hooves, and his hairless hide was near blue in the bright light of noonday. He did not slow his pace, and the rider of the mare, seeing that he was all of metal, backed from out the pass and drew his sword.

Dilvish pulled his own blade from beneath his cloak and parried a head cut as he passed the other rider. Then the man was following after him and crying out:

"Though you have passed the stars of death and leapt the barrier here, you shall never make it to Dilfar! Draw rein! You ride a nether spirit who has taken the form of a horse, but you will be stopped at Mycar or Bildesh—or before!"

But the Colonel of the East did not reply, and Black carried him on with long, effortless strides.

"You ride a mount which never tires," called out the man, "but he is not proof against other sorceries! Give me your sword!"

Dilvish laughed, and his cloak was a wing in the wind.

Before the day lapsed into evening, the mare, too, had fallen, and Dilvish was near Mycar.

Black halted suddenly as they approached the stream called Kethe. Dilvish clung to his neck to keep from being thrown off.

"The bridge is out," said Black, "and I cannot swim."

"Can you clear it?"

"I do not know, my colonel. It is wide. If I cannot clear it, we will never surface again. Kethe cuts deeply into the earth."

And the ambushers came suddenly forth from the trees then, some on horseback and others on foot, the foot soldiers bearing pikes; and Dilvish said: "Try."

3

Black was immediately at full gallop, going faster than horses can run, and the world spun and tumbled about Dilvish as he clung to Black with his knees and his great scarred hands. He cried out as they rose into the air.

When they struck the other bank, Black's hooves sank a full span into the rock and Dilvish reeled in the saddle. He kept his mount, however, and Black freed his hooves.

Looking back at the other bank, Dilvish saw the ambushers standing still, staring at him, then looking down into Kethe, then back up again at him and Black.

As they moved ahead once more, the rider of the piebald stallion fell in beside him and said: "Though you have ridden three horses into the ground, we will stop you between here and Bildesh. Surrender!"

Then Dilvish and Black were far ahead of him, and away.

"They think you are a demon, my mount," he said to Black.

The horse chuckled.

"Perhaps 'twere beter an' I were."

And they rode the sun out of the sky and finally the piebald fell, and the rider cursed Dilvish and Black, and they rode on.

The trees began to fall at Bildesh.

"Deadfalls!" cried Dilvish, but Black was already doing his dance of avoidance and passage. He halted, rearing; and he sprang forward from off his hind legs and passed over a falling log. He halted again and did it once more. Then two fell at once, from opposite sides of the trail, and he leapt backward and then forward again, passing over both.

Two deep pits did he leap across then, and a volley of arrows chattered against his sides, one of them wounding Dilvish in the thigh.

The fifth horseman bore down upon them. The color of fresh-minted gold was this horse, and named Sunset, and his rider was but a youth and light in the saddle,

4

chosen so as to carry the pursuit as far as necessary. He bore a deathlance that shattered against Black's shoulder without causing him to turn. He raced after Dilvish and called out:

"Long have I admired Dilvish, Colonel of the East, so that I do not desire to see him dead. Pray surrender unto me! You will be treated with all courtesies due your station!"

Dilvish did laugh then and made reply, saying:

"Nay, my lad. Better to die than fall to Lylish. On, Black!"

And Black doubled his pace and the boy leaned far forward over Sunset's neck and gave chase. He wore a sword at his side, but he never had chance to use it. Though Sunset ran the entire night, longer and farther than any of the other pursuers, he, too, finally fell as the east began to grow pale.

As he lay there, trying to rise, the youth cried out:

"Though you have escaped me, you shall fall to the Lance!"

Then was Dilvish, called the Damned, riding alone in the hills above Dilfar, bearing his message to that city. And though he rode the horse of steel, called Black, still did he fear an encounter with Lance of the Invincible Armor before he delivered his message.

As he started on the last downward trail his way was blocked a final time, by an armored man on an armored horse. The man held the way completely, and though he was visored, Dilvish knew from his devices that he was Lance, the Right Hand of the Colonel of the West.

"Halt and draw rein, Dilvish!" he called out. "You cannot pass me!"

Lance sat like a statue.

Dilvish halted Black and waited.

"I call upon you to surrender now."

"No," said Dilvish.

"Then must I slay you."

Dilvish drew his sword.

5

The other man laughed.

"Know you not that my armor is unbreachable?"

"No," said Dilvish.

"Very well, then," he said, with something like a chuckle. "We are alone here, you have my word. Dismount. I'll do so at the same time. When you see it is futile, you may have your life. You are my prisoner."

They dismounted.

"You are wounded," said Lance.

Dilvish cut for his neck without replying, hoping to burst the joint. It held, however, and the metal bore not even a scratch to tell of the mighty blow that might have beheaded another.

"You must see now that my armor cannot be breached. It was forged by the Salamanders themselves and bathed in the blood of ten virgins . . ."

Dilvish cut at his head and as he had cut at him, Dilvish had circled slowly to his left, so that now Lance stood with his back to the horse of steel, called Black.

"Now, Black!" cried Dilvish.

Then did Black rear high up on his hind legs and fall forward, bringing his front hooves down toward Lance.

The man called Lance turned rapidly around and they struck him on the chest. He fell.

Two shining hoof marks had been imprinted upon his breastplate.

"You were right," said Dilvish. "It is still unbreached."

Lance moaned again.

". . . And I could slay thee now, with a blade through the eyeslit of thy visor. But I will not, as I did not down thee fairly. When you recover, tell Lylish that Dilfar will be ready for his coming. 'Twere better he withdraw."

"I'll have a sack for thy head when we take the city," said Lance.

"I'll kill thee on the plain before the city," said Dilvish, and he remounted Black and descended the trail, leaving him there on the ground.

And as they rode away, Black said to him: "When you meet, strike at the marks of my hooves. The armor will yield there."

When he came into the city, Dilvish proceeded through the streets to the palace without speaking to those who clustered about him.

He entered the palace and announced himself:

"I am Dilvish, Colonel of the East," he said, "and I am here to report that Portaroy has fallen and is in the hands of Lylish. The armies of the Colonel of the West move in this direction and should be here two days hence. Make haste to arm. Dilfar must not fall."

"Blow then the trumpets," ordered the king, starting from his throne, "and muster the warriors. We must prepare for battle."

And as the trumpets sounded, Dilvish drank him a glass of the good red wine of Dilfar; and as meats and loaves were brought to him, he wondered once again at the strength of Lance's armor and he knew that he must try its invincibility once more.

THELINDE'S
SONG

ACROSS the evening, on the other side of the hill, beneath a moon that was huge and golden, Thelinde was singing.

In the high were-hall of Caer Devash, rung all around with pine trees and mirrored far below its cliffs in that silver river called Denesh, Mildin could hear her daughter's voice and the words of her song:

"The men of Westrim are hardy,
The men of Westrim bold,
But Dilvish who was damned came back
And made their blood run cold.
When they hounded him from Portaroy
To Dilfar in the East,
He rode a thing he'd brought from Hell—
A black and steel beast.
They could not cut nor turn his mount—
The horse that men call Black—
For the colonel gained much wisdom
With the curse of Jelerak—"

Mildin shuddered and fetched her shimmering were-cloak—for she was Mistress of the Coven—and throwing it about her shoulders and clasping it at her neck with the smoky Stone of the Moon, she became as a silver-gray bird and passed out through the window and high about the Denesh.

She crossed over the hill to where Thelinde stood, staring south. Coming to rest upon the lower limb of a nearby tree, she said, through her bird throat: "My child, stop your singing."

"Mother! What is the matter?" asked Thelinde. "Why are you come in swift-form?" And her eyes were full, for they followed the changing of the moon, and in her hair was the silver fire of the witches of the North. She was seventeen and supple, and she loved singing.

"You have sung a name which must not be uttered, even here in the fastness of our keep," said Mildin. "Where did you learn that song?"

"From a thing in the cave," she answered, "where the river called Midnight makes a pool as it passes on its way underground."

"What was the thing in the cave?"

"He is gone by now." Thelinde replied. "He was a

8

dark-traveler, one of the frog kind, I think, who rested there on his way to the Council of Beasts."

"Did he tell you the meaning of that song?" she asked.

"No, he said that it has come but recent, and it is of the wars in the South and the East."

"That is true," said Mildin, "and the frog has no fear of croaking it, for he is of the dark kind and is of no consequence to the mighty. But you, Thelinde, you must be more wary. All of those with power upon them, unless they be rash indeed, fear to mention that name which begins with 'J.'"

"Why is that?"

The silver-gray form fluttered to the ground. Then her mother was standing beside her, tall and pale under the moon; her hair was braided and twisted high upon her head into a crown of the coven, as it is called.

"Come with me now within my cloak, and we will go to the Pool of the Goddess, while the fingers of the moon still touch upon its surface," said Mildin, "and you shall see something of which you have sung."

They descended the hill to the place where the rivulet, which begins high upon the hill at the spring, passes down with barely a ripple into their pool. Mildin knelt beside it in silence, and leaning forward, she breathed upon the surface of the water. Then she summoned Thelinde to her side and they stared downward.

"Look now into the image of the moon reflected in the water," she told her. "Look deeply. Listen . . .

"Long ago," she began, "even as we reckon time, there was a House which was stricken from the peerage of the East, because several generations had intermarried with the Elf-kind. Elfmen are tall and fair to look upon, quick in thought and action, and though their race *is* much older, Men do not generally recognize the Elf peerage. Pity. . . . The last man of this particular House, bereft of his lands and his titles, turned his hand to many occupations, from the sea to

9

the mountains, and finally he came into soldiery, in those first wars with the West, some several centuries ago. Then did he distinguish himself in the great Battle of Portaroy, delivering that city out of the hands of its enemies, so that he came to be called Dilvish the Deliverer. See! The picture comes now clear! It is the entry of Dilvish into Portaroy . . ."

And Thelinde stared into the pool where a picture had formed.

Tall he was, and darker than the Elf-kind, with eyes that laughed and glowed with the pride of triumph. He was mounted on a brown stallion, and his armor, though dented and scratched, still glowed in the morning sun. He rode at the head of his troops, and the people of Portaroy stood at the sides of the roadway and cheered, and the women threw down flowers before him. When he came at last to the fountain in the square, he dismounted and drank the wine of victory. Then the Elders gave speeches of thanks and a great open banquet was laid out for their deliverers.

"He looks to be a good man," said Thelinde. "But what a great sword he wears!—It reaches down to the tops of his boots!"

"Yes, a two-handed engine named that day Deliverer. And his boots, you will note, are of the green Elvish leather, which Men cannot buy—but which are sometimes given as a gift, in sign of favor by the High Ones—and it is said that they leave no footprints. It is a pity that within a sennight of that feast which you see spread, Deliverer should be smashed and Dilvish no longer among the living."

"But he *still* lives!"

"Yes—again."

There was a turbulence within the pool, and another picture emerged.

A dark hillside . . . A man, cloaked and hooded, within a faintly glowing circle . . . A girl bound upon a stone altar . . . A blade in the man's right hand and a staff in his left . . .

10

Mildin felt her daughter's fingers seize upon her shoulder.

"Mother! What is it?"

"It is the One you must never name."

"What is he about?"

"A dark thing, requiring the lifeblood of a virgin. He has waited since beyond time for the stars to re-form themselves into the proper positions for this rite. He has journeyed far, to come to that ancient altar in the hills above Portaroy, to the place where the thing must be accomplished.

"See how the dark things dance about the circle— bats and wraiths and wandering wisps—craving but a drop! They will not touch the circle, though."

"Of course not . . ."

"Now, as the flames of that single brazier reach higher and the stars come into the correct position, he prepares to take her life . . ."

"I cannot watch!"

"Watch!"

"It is the Deliverer, Dilvish, coming that way."

"Yes. After the manner of the High Ones, he seldom sleeps. He goes to take his air in the hills above Portaroy, wearing his full battle trappings as people expect of deliverers."

"He sees Jel— He sees the circle! He advances!"

"Yes, and he breaks the circle. Being of the High Blood, he knows he has ten times the immunity of a man to sorcery. But he does not know whose circle he has broken. Still, it does not kill him. Yet he is weakened—see how he staggers!—so great is the power of that One."

"He strikes the wizard with his hand, knocking him to the ground, and he upsets the brazier. Then he turns to free the girl . . ."

Within the pool, the shadow that was the sorcerer rose from off the ground. His face was invisible within the hood, but he lifted his staff on high. Suddenly he seemed to grow to an enormous height, and his staff

11

lengthened and twisted like a serpent. He reached out and touched the girl, lightly, with its tip.

Thelinde screamed.

Before her eyes the girl was aging. Wrinkles appeared on her face and her hair grew white. Her skin yellowed and her every bone grew prominent beneath it.

Finally she stopped breathing, but the spell did not cease. The thing on the altar shriveled and a fine powder, like smoke, arose from it.

Then a skeleton lay upon the stone.

Dilvish turned upon the sorcerer, raising Deliverer above his shoulder.

But as he brought the blade down, the Dark One touched it with his staff and it shattered and fell at his feet. Then Dilvish advanced one step upon the sorcerer.

Again the staff licked forward, and a nimbus of pale fire played about the form of the Deliverer. After a time it subsided. Still, though, did he stand there, unmoving.

The picture vanished.

"What has happened?"

"The Dark One," said Mildin "wrought him a terrible curse, against which even the High Blood was not proof. Look now."

Day lay upon the hillside. The skeleton lay upon the altar. The sorcerer was gone. Dilvish stood alone, all marble in the sunfall, with the dew of morning upon him, and his right hand was still raised as if to smite an enemy.

Later a group of boys came by and stared for a long while. Then they ran back to the town to tell of it. The Elders of Portaroy came up into the hills, and taking the statue as a gift of the many strange ones who were accounted friends of their Deliverer, they had it carted back to Portaroy and set up in the square beside the fountain.

"He turned him to stone!"

"Yes, and he stood there in the square for over two centuries, his own monument, fist raised against the enemies of the town he had delivered. None ever knew what had become of him, but his human friends grew old and died, and still his statute stood."

". . . And he slept in stone."

"No, the Dark One does not curse that kindly. While his body stood rigid, in full battle trappings, his spirit was banished to one of the deepest pits of Hell the Dark One could manage."

"Oh . . ."

". . . And whether the spell was meant only to be so, or whether the High Blood prevailed in a time of need, or whether some powerful ally of Dilvish's learned the truth and finally worked his release, no one knows. But one day recent, as Lylish, Colonel of the West, swept across the land, all the men Portaroy were assembled in the square preparing defense of the town."

The moon had now crept to the edge of the pool. Beneath it there came another picture:

The men of Portaroy were arming themselves and drilling in the square. They were too few, but they seemed intent upon selling their lives as dearly as possible. Many looked upon the statue of the Deliverer that morning, as though recalling a legend. Then, as the sun wrapped it in color, it moved . . .

For a quarter of an hour, slowly, and with apparent great effort, the limbs changed position. The entire crowd in the square stood and watched, itself unmoving now. Finally Dilvish climbed down from his pedestal and drank from the fountain.

The people were all around him then, and he turned toward them.

"His eyes, mother! They have changed!"

"After what he has seen with the eyes of his spirit, is it a wonder that the outer ones reflect it?"

The picture vanished. The moon swam farther away.

". . . And from somewhere he got him a horse that was not a horse, but a beast of steel in the likeness of a horse."

For a moment a dark and running form appeared within the pool.

"That is Black, his mount. Dilvish rode him into

the battle, and though he fought long on foot, too, he rode him out again, much later—the only survivor. In the weeks before the battle he had trained his men well, but they were too few. He was named Colonel of the East by them, in opposition to the title Lord Lylish wears. All fell, however, save he, though the lords and elders of the other cities of the East have now risen in arms and they, too, recognize his rank. This very day, I have been told, he stood before the walls of Dilfar and slew Lance of the Invincible Armor in single combat. But the moon falls now and the water darkens . . ."

"But the name? Why must I not mention the name of Jelerak?"

As she spoke it, there came a rustling sound, as of great dry wings beating at the air overhead, and the moon was obscured by a cloud, and a dark shape was reflected deep within the pool.

Mildin drew her daughter within the were-cloak.

The rustling grew louder and a faint mist sprang up about them.

Mildin made the Sign of the Moon, and she began to speak softly:

"Back with thee—in the Name of the Coven, of which I am Mistress, I charge thee return. Go back where thou camest. We desire not thy dark wings above Caer Devash."

There was a downdraft of air, and a flat expressionless face hovered just above them, couched between wide bat wings. Its talons were faintly glowing, red, as of metal just heated at the forge.

It circled them, and Mildin drew the cloak tighter and raised her hand.

"By the Moon, our Mother, in all her guises, I charge thee depart. Now! This instant! Get away from Caer Devash!"

It landed upon the ground beside them, but Mildin's cloak began to glow and the Stone of the Moon blazed like a milky flame. It drew back from the light, back within the mists.

14

Then an opening appeared in the cloud and a shaft of moonlight passed through it. A single moonbeam touched upon the creature.

It screamed once, like a man in great pain, then mounted into the air heading southwest.

Thelinde looked up into her mother's face, which suddenly appeared very tried, older . . .

"What was it?" she asked her.

"It was a servant of the Dark One. I tried to warn you, in the most graphic way possible, of his power. For so long has his name been used in the conjuring and compelling of fell spirits and dark wights that his has become a Name of Power. They rush to find the speaker, whenever they hear it uttered, lest it should be he and he should grow angry at their tardiness. If it is not he, they often seek vengeance upon the presumptuous speaker. It is also said, though, that if his name be pronounced too often by one person, then he himself becomes aware of this and sends a doom upon that person. Either way, it is not wise to go about singing such songs."

"I will not, ever. How can a sorcerer be that strong?"

"He is as old as the hills. He was once a white wizard and he fell into dark ways, which makes him particularly malicious—you know, they seldom ever change for the better—and he is now accounted to be one of the three most powerful, possibly *the* most powerful, of all the wizards in all the kingdoms of all the Earths. He is still alive and very strong, though the story which you saw took place centuries ago. But even he is not without his problems . . ."

"Why is that?" asked the witch's daughter.

"Because Dilvish is come alive once more, and I believe he is somewhat angry."

The moon emerged from behind the cloud, and huge it was, and it had turned to fallow gold during its absence.

Mildin and her daughter headed back up the hill then, toward Caer Devash rung round with pines, high above Denesh, the silver river.

THE BELLS
OF SHOREDAN

No living thing dwelled in the land of Rahoringhast.

Since an age before this age had the dead realm been empty of sound, save for the crashing of thunders and the *spit-spit* of raindrops ricocheting from off its stonework and the stones. The towers of the Citadel of Rahoring still stood; the great archway from which the gates had been stricken continued to gape, like a mouth frozen in a howl of pain and surprise, of death; the countryside about the place resembled the sterile landscape of the moon.

The rider followed the Way of the Armies, which led at last to the archway, and on through into the Citadel. Behind him lay a twisted trail leading downward, downward, and back, toward the south and the west. It ran through chill patterns of morning mist that clung, swollen, to dark and pitted ground, like squadrons of gigantic leeches. It looped about the ancient towers, still standing only by virtue of enchantments placed upon them in foregone days. Black and awesome, high rearing, and limned in nightmare's clarity, the towers and the citadel were the final visible extensions of the character of their dead maker: Hohorga, King of the World.

The rider, the green-booted rider who left no footprints when he walked, must have felt something of the

16

dark power that still remained within the place, for he halted and sat silent, staring for a long while at the broken gates and the high battlements. Then he spoke a word to the black, horselike thing he rode upon, and they pressed ahead.

As he drew near, he saw that something was moving in the shadows of the archway.

He knew that no living thing dwelled in the land of Rahoringhast . . .

The battle had gone well, considering the number of the defenders.

On the first day, the emissaries of Lylish had approached the walls of Dilfar, sought parley, requested surrender of the city, and been refused. There followed a brief truce to permit single combat between Lance, the Hand of Lylish, and Dilvish called the Damned, Colonel of the East, Deliverer of Portaroy, scion of the Elvish House of Selar and the human House that hath been stricken.

The trial lasted but a quarter of an hour, until Dilvish, whose wounded leg had caused his collapse, did strike upward from behind his buckler with the point of his blade. The armor of Lance, which had been deemed invincible, gave way then, when the blade of Dilvish smote at one of the two devices upon the breastplate—those that were cast in the form of cloven hoof marks. Men muttered that these devices had not been present previously and an attempt was made to take the colonel prisoner. His horse, however, which had stood on the sidelines like a steel statue, did again come to his aid, bearing him to safety within the city.

The assault was then begun, but the defenders were prepared and held well their walls. Well fortified and well provided was Dilfar. Fighting from a position of strength, the defenders cast down much destruction upon the men of the West.

After four days the army of Lylish had withdrawn with the great rams that it had been unable to use. The men of the West commenced the construction of helepoles, while they awaited the arrival of catapults from Bildesh.

Above the walls of Dilfar, high in the Keep of Eagles, there were two who watched.

"It will not go well, Lord Dilvish," said the king, whose name was Malacar the Mighty, though he was short of stature and long of year. "If they complete the towers-that-walk and bring catapults, they will strike us from afar. We will not be able to defend against this. Then the towers will walk when we are weakened from the bombardment."

"It is true," said Dilvish.

"Dilfar must not fall."

"No."

"Reinforcements have been sent for, but they are many leagues distant. None were prepared for the assault of Lord Lylish, and it will be long before sufficient troops will be mustered and be come here to the battle."

"That is also true, and by then may it be too late."

"You are said by some to be the same Lord Dilvish who liberated Portaroy in days long gone by."

"I am that Dilvish."

"If so, that Dilvish was of the House of Selar of the Invisible Blade."

"Yes."

"Is it true also, then—what is told of the House of Selar and the bells of Shoredan in Rahoringhast?"

Malacar looked away as he said it.

"This thing I do not know," said Dilvish. "I have never attempted to raise the cursed legions of Shoredan. My grandmother told me that only twice in all the ages of Time has this been done. I have also read of it in the Green Books of Time at the keep of Mirata. I do not *know*, however."

"Only to one of the House of Selar will the bells respond. Else they swing noiseless, it is said."

"So is it said."

"Rahoringhast lies far to the north and east, and distressful is the way. One with a mount such as yours

18

might make the journey, might ring there the bells, might call forth the doomed legions, though. It is said they will follow such a one of Selar to battle."

"Aye, this thought has come to me, also."

"Willst essay this thing?"

"Aye, sir. Tonight. I am already prepared."

"Kneel then and receive thou my blessing, Dilvish of Selar. I knew thou wert he when I saw thee on the field before these walls."

And Dilvish did kneel and receive the blessing of Malacar, called the Mighty, Liege of the Eastern Reach, whose realm held Dilfar, Bildesh, Maestar, Mycar, Portaroy, Princeaton, and Poind.

The way was difficult, but the passage of leagues and hours was as the movement of clouds. The western portal to Dilfar had within it a smaller passing-place, a man-sized door studded with spikes and slitted for the discharge of bolts.

Like a shutter in the wind, this door opened and closed. Crouched low, mounted on a piece of the night, the colonel passed out through the opening and raced across the plain, entering for a moment the outskirts of the enemy camp.

A cry went up as he rode, and weapons rattled in the darkness.

Sparks flew from unshod steel hooves.

"All the speed at thy command now, Black, my mount!"

He was through the campsite and away before arrow could be set to bow.

High on the hill to the east, a small fire throbbed in the wind. Pennons, mounted on tall poles, flopped against the night, and it was too dark for Dilvish to read the devices thereon, but he knew that they stood before the tents of Lylish, Colonel of the West.

Dilvish spoke the words in the language of the damned, and as he spoke them the eyes of his mount glowed like embers in the night. The small fire on the hilltop leapt, one great leaf of flame, to the height of four men. It did not reach the tent, however. Then there was no fire at all, only the embers of all the fuels consumed in a single moment.

Dilvish rode on, and the hooves of Black made lightning on the hillside.

They pursued him a small while only. Then he was away and alone.

All that night did he ride through places of rock. Shapes reared high above him and fell again, like staggering giants surprised in their drunkenness. He felt himself launched, countless times, through empty air, and when he looked down on these occasions, there was only empty air beneath him.

With the morning, there came a leveling of his path, and the far edge of the Eastern Plain lay before him, then under him. His leg began to throb beneath its dressing, but he had lived in the Houses of Pain for more than the lifetimes of Men, and he put the feeling far from his thoughts.

After the sun had raised itself over the jagged horizon at his back, he stopped to eat and to drink, to stretch his limbs.

In the sky then he saw the shapes of the nine black doves that must circle the world forever, never to land, seeing all things on the earth and on the sea, and passing all things by.

"An omen," he said. "Be it a good one?"

"I know not," replied the creature of steel.

"Then let us make haste to learn."

He remounted.

For four days did he pass over the plain, until the yellow and green waving grasses gave way and the land lay sandy before him.

The winds of the desert cut at his eyes. He fixed his scarf as a muffle, but it could not stop the entire assault. When he would cough and spit, he needed to lower it, and the sand entered again. He would blink and his face would burn, and he would curse, but no spell he knew could lay the entire desert like yellow tapestry, smooth and unruffled below him. Black was an opposing wind, and the airs of the land rushed to contest his passage.

On the third day in the desert, a mad wight flew invisible and gibbering at his back. Even Black could not outrun it, and it ignored the foulest imprecations of Mabrahoring, language of the demons and the damned.

The following day, more joined with it. They would not pass the protective circle in which Dilvish slept, but they screamed across his dreams—meaningless fragments of a dozen tongues—troubling his sleep.

He left them when he left the desert. He left them as he entered the land of stone and marches and gravel and dark pools and evil openings in the ground from which the fumes of the underworld came forth.

He had come to the border of Rahoringhast.

It was damp and gray, everywhere.

It was misty in places, and the water oozed forth from the rocks, came up from out of the ground.

There were no trees, shrubs, flowers, grasses. No birds sang, no insects hummed. . . . No living thing dwelled in the land of Rahoringhast.

Dilvish rode on and entered through the broken jaws of the city.

All within was shadow and ruin.

He passed up the Way of the Armies.

Silent was Rahoringhast, a city of the dead.

He could feel this, not as the silence of nothingness now, but as the silence of a still presence.

Only the steel cloven hooves sounded within the city. There came no echoes.

Sound . . . Nothing. Sound . . . Nothing. Sound . . .

It was as though something unseen moved to absorb every evidence of life as soon as it noised itself.

Red was the palace, like bricks hot from the kiln and flushed with the tempers of their making. But of one piece were the walls. No seams, no divisions were there in the sheet of red. It was solid, was imponderable, broad of base, and reached with its thirteen towers higher than any building Dilvish had ever seen, though he had dwelled in the high keep of Mirata itself, where the Lords of Illusion hold sway, bending space to their will.

Dilvish dismounted and regarded the enormous stairway that lay before him. "That which we seek lies within."

Black nodded and touched the first stair with his hoof. Fire rose from the stone. He drew back his hoof and smoke curled about it. There was no mark upon the stair to indicate where he had touched.

"I fear I cannot enter this place and preserve my form," he stated. "At the least, my form."

"What compels thee?"

"An ancient enchantment to preserve this place against the assault of any such as I."

"Can it be undone?"

"Not by any creature which walks this world or flies above it or writhes beneath it or I'm a horse. Though the seas some day rise and cover the land, this place will exist at their bottom. This was torn from Chaos by Order in the days when those principles stalked the land, naked, just beyond the hills. Whoever compelled them was one of the First, and powerful even in terms of the Mighty."

"Then I must go alone."

"Perhaps not. One is approaching even now with whom you had best wait and parley."

Dilvish waited, and a single horseman emerged from a distant street and advanced upon them.

"Greetings," called the rider, raising his right hand, open.

"Greetings." Dilvish returned the gesture.

The man dismounted. His costume was deep violet in color, the hood thrown back, the cloak all engulfing. He bore no visible arms.

"Why stand you here before the Citadel of Rahoring?" he asked.

"Why stand you here to ask me, priest of Babrigore?" said Dilvish, and not ungently.

"I am spending the time of a moon in this place of death, to dwell upon the ways of evil. It is to prepare myself as head of my temple."

22

"You are young to be head of a temple."

The priest shrugged and smiled.

"Few come to Rahoringhast," he observed.

"Small wonder," did Dilvish reply. "I trust I shall not remain here long."

"Were you planning on entering this—place?" He gestured.

"I was, and am."

The man was half a head shorter than Dilvish, and it was impossible to guess at his form beneath the robes he wore. His eyes were blue and he was swarthy of complexion. A mole on his left eyelid danced when he blinked.

"Let me beg you reconsider this action," he stated. "It would be unwise to enter this building."

"Why is that?"

"It is said that it is still guarded within by the ancient warders of its lord."

"Have you ever been inside?"

"Yes."

"Were you troubled by any ancient wardens?"

"No, but as a priest of Babrigore I am under the protection of—of—Jelerak."

Dilvish spat.

"May his flesh be flayed from his bones and his life yet remain."

The priest dropped his eyes.

"Though he fought the creature which dwelled within this place," said Dilvish, "he became as foul himself afterward."

"Many of his deeds do lie like stains upon the land," said the priest, "but he was not always such a one. He was a white wizard who matched his powers against the Dark One, in days when the world was young. He was not sufficient. He fell. He was taken as servant by the Maleficient. For centuries he endured this bondage, until it changed him, as such must. He, too, came to glory in the ways of darkness. But then, when Selar of the Unseen Blade bought the life of Hohorga with his own, Jel—he fell as if dead and lay as such for

23

the space of a week. Near delirious, when he awakened, he worked with counterspell at one last act of undoing: to free the cursed legions of Shoredan. He essayed that thing. He did. He stood upon this very stairway for two days and two nights, until the blood mingled with perspiration on his brow, but he could not break the hold of Hohorga. Even dead, the dark strength was too great for him. Then he wandered mad about the countryside, until he was taken in and cared for by the priests of Babrigore. Afterward he lapsed back into the ways he had learned, but he has always been kindly disposed toward the Order which cared for him. He has never asked anything more of us. He has sent us food in times of famine. Speak no evil of him in my presence."

Dilvish spat again.

"May he thrash in the darkness of the darknesses for the ages of ages, and may his name be cursed forever."

The priest looked away from the sudden blaze in his eyes.

"What want you in Rahoring?" he asked finally.

"To go within—and do a thing."

"If you must, then I shall accompany you. Perhaps my protection shall also extend to yourself."

"I do not solicit your protection, priest."

"The asking is not necessary."

"Very well. Come with me then."

He started up the stairway.

"What is that thing you ride?" asked the priest, gesturing back. "—Like a horse in form, but now it is a statue."

Dilvish laughed.

"I, too, know something of the ways of darkness, but my terms with it are my own."

"No man may have special terms with darkness."

"Tell it to a dweller in the Houses of Pain, priest. Tell it to a statue. Tell it to one who is all of the race of Men! Tell it not to me."

"What is your name?"

"Dilvish. What is yours?"

"Korel. I shall speak to you no more of darkness then, Dilvish, but I will still go with you into Ra-horing."

"Then stand not talking." Dilvish turned and continued upward.

Korel followed him.

When they had gone halfway, the daylight began to grow dim about them. Dilvish looked back. All he could see was the stairway leading down and down, back. There was nothing else in the world but the stairs. With each step upward, the darkness grew.

"Did it happen thus when last you entered this place?" he asked.

"No," said Korel.

They reached the top of the stairs and stood before the dim portal. By then it was as though night lay upon the land.

They entered.

A sound, as of music, came far ahead and there was a flickering light within. Dilvish laid his hand upon the hilt of his sword. The priest whispered to him: "It will do you no good."

They moved up the passageway and came at length into a vacant hall. Braziers spewed flame from high sockets in the walls. The ceiling was lost in shadow and smoke.

They crossed that hall to where a wide stair led up into a blaze of light and sound.

Korel looked back.

"It begins with the light," said he, "all this newness" —gesturing. "The outer passage bore only rubble and . . . dust . . ."

"What else is the matter?" Dilvish looked back.

Only one set of footprints led into the hall through the dust. Dilvish then laughed, saying: "I tread lightly."

Korel studied him. Then he blinked and his mole jerked across his eye.

"When I entered here before," he said, "there were no sounds, no torches. Everything lay empty and still, ruined. Do you know what is happening?"

"Yes," said Dilvish, "for I read of it in the Green Books of Time at the keep of Mirata. Know, O priest of Babrigore, that within the hall above the ghosts do play at being ghosts. Know, too, that Hohorga dies again and again so long as I stand within this place."

As he spoke the name Hohorga a great cry was heard within the high hall. Dilvish raced up the stairs, the priest rushing after him.

Now within the halls of Rahoring there came up a mighty wailing.

They stood at the top of the stairs, Dilvish like a statue, blade half drawn from its sheath; Korel, hands within his sleeves, praying after the manner of his order.

The remains of a great feast were strewn about the hall; the light came down out of the air from colored globes that circled like planets through the great heaven-design within the vaulted ceiling; the throne on the high dais beside the far wall was empty. That throne was too large for any of this age to occupy. The walls were covered all over with ancient devices, strange, on alternate slabs of white and orange marble. In the pillars of the wall were set gems the size of doubled fists, burning yellow and emerald, infraruby and ultrablue, casting a fire radiance, transparent and illuminating, as far as the steps to the throne. The canopy of the throne was wide and all of white gold, worked in the manner of mermaids and harpies, dolphins and goat-headed snakes; it was supported by wyvern, hippogriff, firedrake, chimera, unicorn, cockatrice, griffin, and pegasus, sejant erect. It belonged to the one who lay dying upon the floor.

In the form of a man, but half again as large, Hohorga lay upon the tiles of his palace and his intestines filled his lap. He was supported by three of his guard, while the rest attended to his slayer. It had been said in the Books of Time that Hohorga the Maleficent was indescribable. Dilvish saw that this was both true and untrue.

He was fair to look upon and noble of feature; but so blindingly fair was he that all eyes were averted from

26

that countenance now lined with pain. A faint bluish halo was diminishing about his shoulders. Even in the death pain he was as cold and perfect as a carved gem-stone, set upon the red-green cushion of his blood; his was the hypnotic perfection of a snake of many colors. It is said that eyes have no expression of their own, and that one could not reach into a barrel of eyes and separate out those of an angry man or those of one's beloved. Hohorga's eyes were the eyes of a ruined god: infinitely sad, as proud as an ocean of lions.

One look and Dilvish knew this thing, though he could not tell their color.

Hohorga was of the blood of the First.

The guards had cornered the slayer. He fought them, apparently empty-handed, but parrying and thrusting as though he gripped a blade. Wherever his hand moved, there were wounds.

He wielded the only weapon that might have slain the King of the World, who permitted none to go armed in his presence save his own guard.

He bore the Invisible Blade.

He was Selar, first of the Elvish house of that name, great-gone-sire of Dilvish, who at that moment cried out his name.

Dilvish drew his blade and rushed across the hall. He cut at the attackers, but his blade passed through them as through smoke.

They beat down Selar's guard. A mighty blow sent something unseen ringing across the hall. Then they dismembered him, slowly, Selar of Shoredan, as Dilvish wept, watching.

And then Hohorga spoke, in a voice held firm though soft, without inflection, like the steady beating of surf or the hooves of horses:

"I have outlived the one who presumed to lay hands upon me, which is as it must be. Know that it was written that eyes would never see the blade that could slay me. Thus do the powers have their jokes. Much of what I have done shall never be undone, O children of Men and Elves and Salamanders. Much more than

27

you know do I take with me from this world into the silence. You have slain that which was greater than yourselves, but do not be proud. It matters no longer to me. Nothing does. Have my curses."

Those eyes closed and there was a clap of thunder.

Dilvish and Korel stood alone in the darkened ruins of a great hall.

"Why did this thing appear today?" asked the priest.

"When one of the blood of Selar enters here," said Dilvish, "it is reenacted."

"Why have you come here, Dilvish, son of Selar?"

"To ring the bells of Shoredan."

"It cannot be."

"If I am to save Dilfar and redeliver Portaroy it *must* be.

"I go now to seek the bells," he said.

He crossed through the near blackness of night without stars, for neither were his eyes the eyes of Men, and he was accustomed to much dark.

He heard the priest following after him.

They circled behind the broken bulk of the Earth Lord's throne. Had there been sufficient light as they passed, they would have seen darkened spots upon the floor turning to stain, then crisp sand-brown, and then to red-green blood, as Dilvish moved near them, and vanishing once again as he moved away.

Behind the dais was the door to the central tower. Fevera Mirata, Queen of Illusion, had once shown Dilvish this hall in a mirror the size of six horsemen riding abreast, and broidered about with a frame of golden daffodils that hid their heads till it cleared of all save their reflections.

Dilvish opened the door and halted. Smoke billowed forth, engulfing him. He was seized with coughing but he kept his guard before him.

"It is the Warden of the Bells!" cried Korel. "Jelerak deliver us!"

"Damn Jelerak!" said Dilvish. "I'll deliver myself."

But as he spoke, the cloud swirled away and spun itself into a glowing tower that held the doorway, illuminating the throne and the places about the throne. Two red eyes glowed within the smoke.

Dilvish passed his blade through and through the cloud, meeting with no resistance.

"If you remain incorporeal, I shall pass through you," he called out. "If you take a shape, I shall dismember it. Make your choice," and he said it in Mabrahoring, the language spoken in Hell.

"Deliverer, Deliverer, Deliverer," hissed the cloud, "my pet Dilvish, little creature of hooks and chains. Do you not know your master? Is your memory so short?" And the cloud collapsed upon itself and coalesced into a bird-headed creature with the hindquarters of a lion and two serpents growing up from its shoulders, curling and engendering about its high crest of flaming quills.

"Cal-den!"

"Aye, your old tormenter, Elf man. I have missed you, for few depart my care. It is time you returned."

"This time," said Dilvish, "I am not chained and unarmed, and we meet in my world," and he cut forward with his blade, striking the serpent head from Cal-den's left shoulder.

A piercing bird cry filled the hall and Cal-den sprang forward.

Dilvish struck at his breast but the blade was turned aside, leaving only a smallish gash from which a pale liquor flowed.

Cal-den struck him then backward against the dais, catching his blade in a black claw, shattering it, and he raised his other arm to smite him. Dilvish did then stab upward with what remained of the sword, nine inches of jagged length.

It caught Cal-den beneath the jaw, entering there and remaining, the hilt torn from Dilvish's hand as the tormentor shook his head, roaring.

Then was Dilvish seized about the waist so that his bones did sigh and creak within him. He felt himself raised into the air, the serpent tearing at his ear, claws piercing his sides. Cal-den's face was turned up toward him, wearing the hilt of his blade like a beard of steel.

29

Then did he hurl Dilvish across the dais, so as to smash him against the tiles of the floor.

But the wearer of the green boots of Elfland may not fall or be thrown to land other than on his feet.

Dilvish did recover him then, but the shock of his landing caused pain in the thigh wound he bore. His leg collapsed beneath him, so that he put out his hand to the side.

Cal-den did then spring upon him, smiting him sorely about the head and shoulders. From somewhere Korel hurled a stone that struck upon the demon's crest.

Dilvish came scrambling backward, until his hand came upon a thing in the rubble that drew the blood from it.

A blade.

He snatched at the hilt and brought it up off the floor with a side-armed cut that struck Cal-den across the back, stiffening him into a bellow that near burst the ears to hear. Smoke rose from the wound.

Dilvish stood, and saw that he held nothing.

Then did he know that the blade of his ancestor, which no eyes may look upon, had come to him from the ruins, where it had lain across the ages, to serve him, scion of the House of Selar, in this moment of his need.

He directed it toward the breast of Cal-den.

"My rabbit, you are unarmed, yet you have cut me," said the creature. "Now shall we return to the Houses of Pain."

They both lunged forward.

"I always knew," said Cal-den, "that my little Dilvish was something special," and he fell to the floor with an enormous crash and the smokes arose from his body.

Dilvish placed his heel upon the carcass and wrenched free the blade outlined in steaming ichor.

"To you, Selar, do I owe this victory," he said, and raised a length of smouldering nothingness in salute. Then he sheathed the sword.

Korel was at his side. He watched as the creature

30

at their feet vanished like embers and ice, leaving behind a stench that was most foul to smell.

Dilvish turned him again to the door of the tower and entered there, Korel at his side.

The broken bellpull lay at his feet. It fell to dust when he touched it with his toe.

"It is said," he told Korel, "that the bellpull did break in the hands of the last to ring it, half an age ago."

He raised his eye, and there was only darkness above him.

"The legions of Shoredan did set forth to assault the Citadel of Rahoring," said the priest, as though reading it from some old parchment, "and word of their movement came soon to the King of the World. Then did he lay upon three bells cast in Shoredan a weird. When these bells were rung, a great fog came over the land and engulfed the columns of marchers and those on horseback. The fog did disperse upon the second ringing of the bells, and the land was found to be empty of the troop. It was later written by Merde, Red Wizard of the South, that somewhere still do these marchers and horsemen move, through regions of eternal fog. 'If these bells be rung again by a hand of that House which dispatched the layer of the weird, then will these legions come forth from a mist to serve that one for a time in battle. But when they have served, they will vanish again into the places of gloom, where they will continue their march upon a Rahoringhast which no longer exists. How they may be freed to rest, this thing is not known. One mightier than I has tried and failed.' "

Dilvish bowed his head a moment, then he felt the walls. They were not like the outer walls. They were cast of blocks of that same material, and between those blocks were scant crevices wherein his fingers found purchase.

He raised himself above the floor and commenced to climb, the soft green boots somehow finding toeholds wherever they struck.

The air was hot and stale, and showers of dust de-

31

scended upon him each time he raised an arm above his head.

He pulled himself upward, until he counted a hundred such movements and the nails of his hands were broken. Then he clung to the wall like a lizard, resting, and felt the pains of his last encounter burning like suns within him.

He breathed the fetid air and his head swam. He thought of the Portaroy he had once delivered, long ago, the city of friends, the place where he had once been feted, the land whose need for him had been strong enough to free him from the Houses of Pain and break the grip of stone upon his body; and he thought of that Portaroy in the hands of the Colonel of the West, and he thought of Dilfar now resisting that Lylish who might sweep the bastions of the East before him.

He climbed once again.

His head touched the metal lip of a bell.

He climbed around it, bracing himself on the crossbars that now occurred.

There were three bells suspended from a single axle.

He set his back against the wall and clung to the crossbars, placing his feet upon the middle bell.

He pushed, straightening his legs.

The axle protested, creaking and grinding within its sockets.

But the bell moved, slowly. It did not return, however, but stayed in the position into which it had been pushed.

Cursing, he worked his way through the crossbars and over to the opposite side of the belfry.

He pushed it back and it stuck on the other side. All the bells moved with the axle, though.

Nine times more did he cross over in darkness to push at the bells.

Then they moved more easily.

Slowly they fell back as he released the pressure of his legs. He pushed them out again and they returned again. He pushed them again, and again.

A click came from one of the bells as the clapper struck. Then another. Finally one of them rang.

He kicked out harder and harder, and then did the bells swing free and fill the tower about him with a pealing that vibrated the roots of his teeth and filled his ears with pain. A storm of dust came down over him and his eyes were full of tears. He coughed and closed them. He let the bells grow still.

Across some mighty distance he thought he heard the faint winding of a horn.

He began the downward climb.

"Lord Dilvish," said Korel, when he had reached the floor, "I have heard the blowing of horns."

"Yes," said Dilvish.

"I have a flask of wine with me. Drink."

Dilvish rinsed his mouth and spat, then drank three mighty swallows.

"Thank you, priest. Let us be gone from here now."

They crossed through the hall once more and descended the inner stairs. The smaller hall was now unlighted and lay in ruin. They made their way out, Dilvish leaving no tracks to show where he had gone; and halfway down the stairs the darkness departed from them.

Through the bleak day that now clung to the land, Dilvish looked back along the Way of the Armies. A mighty fog filled the air far beyond the broken gates, and from within that fog there came again the notes of the horn and the sounds of the movements of troops. Almost, Dilvish could see the outlines of the columns of marchers and riders, moving, moving, but not advancing.

"My troops await me," said Dilvish upon the stair. "Thank you, Korel, for accompanying me."

"Thank you, Lord Dilvish. I came to this place to dwell upon the ways of evil. You have shown me much that I may meditate upon."

They descended the final stairs. Dilvish brushed dust from his garments and mounted Black.

"One thing more, Korel, priest of Babrigore," he

33

said. "If you ever meet with your patron, who should provide you much more evil to meditate upon than you have seen here, tell him that, when all the battles have been fought, his statue will come to kill him."

The mole danced as Korel blinked up at him.

"Remember," he replied, "that once he wore a mantle of light."

Dilvish laughed, and the eyes of his mount glowed red through the gloom.

"There!" he said, gesturing. "There is your sign of his goodness and light!"

Nine black doves circled in the heavens.

Korel bowed his head and did not answer.

"I go now to lead my legions."

Black reared on steel hooves and laughed along with his rider.

Then they were gone, up the Way of the Armies, leaving the Citadel of Rahoring and the priest of Babrigore behind them in the gloom.

A KNIGHT
FOR MERYTHA

As he rode through the pass, he heard a woman scream.

The scream echoed about him and died. Then there was only the sound of the steel hooves of his mount upon the trail.

He stopped and stared through the gathering dusk.

"Black, whence came that cry?" he asked.

"I know not the direction," replied the steel horse on whose back he rode. "In these mountains sounds seem to come from everywhere."

Dilvish turned on his saddle and stared back along the trail he had followed.

Far below him on the plain, the doomed army had made its camp. Dilvish, who slept but little, had ridden ahead to scout out the way into the mountains. When last he had passed here, on the way to Rahoringhast, it had been at night and he had seen little of the trail.

Black's eyes glowed faintly.

"The darkness increases," he said, "and 'tis profitless to proceed. You cannot see much of the way beyond this point. Perhaps 'twere better you returned now to the camp, to hear your ancient kinsmen's tales of younger days in the earth."

"Very well . . ." said Dilvish, and as he spoke these words the cry came once more.

"That way!" he said, gesturing to his left. "The cry came from up ahead, off the trail!"

"Yes," said Black, "we are near enough to the borders of Rahoringhast so that a situation such as this is even more suspect than it normally would be. I counsel you not to heed that cry."

"A woman screaming in the wilderness and night— and I not responding? Come now, Black! It violates the law of my kind. Onward!"

Black made a sound like the hunting cry of a great bird and leapt forward. Beyond the pass he turned off the trail and ascended a steep slope.

High above there was a flicker of light.

"It is a castle," said Black, "and a woman stands within the battlement, all in white."

Dilvish stared ahead.

The clouds parted and the moon dropped light upon the edifice.

Big, and in places lapsing into ruin, it seemed almost a part of the mountainside. Dark, save for a faint illumination coming through the opened gate from the courtyard within. Old . . .

They came to the walls of the castle and Dilvish called out:

"Lady! Was it you who screamed?"

She looked downward.

"Yes!" she said. "Oh yes, good traveler! 'Twas I."

"What troubles you, madam?"

"I called out because I heard you passing. There is a dragon in the courtyard—and I fear for my life."

"Did you say 'dragon'?"

"Yes, good sir. He came down out of the sky four days ago and has been making his new home here. I am a prisoner because of this. I cannot pass that way . . ."

"I will see what can be done about it," he said.

Dilvish drew his invisible blade.

"Oh, good sir . . ."

"Through the gate, Black!"

"I like it not," muttered Black as they clattered into the courtyard.

Dilvish looked about him.

A torch blazed at one end of the yard. Shadows danced everywhere. Otherwise there was nothing.

"I see no dragon," said Black.

"And I smell no reptilian musk."

"Here, dragon!" said Black. "Here, dragon! Come on, dragon!"

They circled the courtyard, peering through the archways.

"No dragon," Black observed.

"No."

"Pity. You must forgo the pleasure."

As they passed a final archway, the woman called out from within.

"It appears to have departed, good sir."

He sheathed the blade of Selar and dismounted. Black became a steel statue at his back as he strode through the archway. The woman stood before him and he smiled and bowed to her.

"Your dragon appears to have flown," he observed. Then he stared at her.

Her hair was black and unbraided, falling far below her shoulders. She was tall, and her eyes were the color of wood smoke. Rubies danced upon the lobes of her ears, and her chin was tiny and she held it high. Her neck was the color of cream, and Dilvish ran his eyes along it, down to the slopes where her breasts fitted into the tight bodice of her dress.

"So it would seem," she said. "My name is Merytha."

". . . And mine is Dilvish."

"You are a brave man, Dilvish—to rush empty-handed after a dragon."

"Perhaps," he said. "Since the dragon is now departed . . ."

"It will be back for me, I fear," she said, "for I am the last one within these walls."

"Alone here? What is your situation?"

"My kinsmen will return tomorrow. They have been on a far journey. Pray, tend your horse and come dine with me, for I am lonesome and afraid." She licked her lips into a smile, and Dilvish said, "Very well," and he returned to the courtyard.

He placed his hand on Black's neck and felt it move.

"Black, all is not right in this place," he stated, "and I would learn more of it. I go to dine with the lady."

"Take care," whispered Black, "of what you eat and drink. I do not like this place."

"Good Black," said Dilvish, and he returned to Merytha within the archway.

She had obtained a lighted torch from somewhere, which she handed to him.

"My chambers are at the head of the stairs," she said.

He followed her upward through the gloom. Cobwebs hung in the corners and there was dust upon a wide tapestry that depicted a vast battle. He thought he heard the scurry of rats within the rushes, and a faint odor of dry rot came to his nostrils.

They reached a landing and she pushed wide the door that was before them.

The room was lighted by many tapers. It was clean and warm, and an aroma of sandlewood hung in the air. There were dark animal pelts upon the floor, and a bright tapestry hung on the far wall. Two windowslits let in the night breeze and glimpses of the stars, and there was a narrow doorway that led out to the battlement from which she had hailed him.

Dilvish moved into the room, and as he did so he saw that beyond the corner to his left there was a recessed fireplace, two logs smouldering within it. Laid out on the table before the hearth was a meal. Vegetables still steamed beside the the beef, and the bread looked soft and fresh. There was a clear decanter of red wine. In the corner of the room, he saw a massive, canopied bed, great ropes of golden braid about its posts, orange silk stretched tight upon it where the coverlet was turned back, and a row of orange pillows at its head.

"Sit down and refresh yourself, Dilvish," said Merytha.

"Will you not eat with me?"

"I have already dined."

Dilvish tasted a small piece of beef. There was no taint to it. He sipped the wine. It was strong and dry.

"Very good," he said. "How did this meal come to be prepared, and still warm?"

She smiled. "I did it, perhaps in anticipation. Will you not remove your sword belt at my table?"

"Yes," he replied. "Excuse me."

And he unbuckled it and placed it beside him.

"You carry no blade in your scabbard. Why is that?"

"Mine was broken in battle."

"You still must have won the engagement, else you would not be here."

"I won," said Dilvish.

"I take you for a doughty warrior, sir."

He smiled.

"The lady will turn my head with such talk."

She laughed.

"May I play music for you?"

"That would be pleasant."

She fetched then a stringed instrument unlike any he had ever seen. She began to play it and to sing:

"The wind doth blow this night, my love,
  And a few small drops of rain;
I prayed that thou wouldst come to me,
  To ease me of my pain.

Now I wish the wind may never cease,
  Nor the flashes in the flood,
That thou has come across the eve
  In earthly flesh and blood.

I prithee stay, of goodly night,
  Green boots upon thy feet,
O knight who does not wear a sword,
  To close my eyes with kisses sweet.

I'll wish the wind may never cease,
  Nor flashes in the flood,
That thou mightst stay across the eve,
  In earthly flesh and blood.

I prayed that thou wouldst come to me
  As the light of day did wane,
To hold me as the night wind blew,
  And a few small drops of rain."

Dilvish ate and drank his wine, watching her as she played. Her fingers barely touched upon the strings and her voice was soft and clear.

"Lovely," he said.

"Thank you, Dilvish," and she sang him another tune.

He finished his meal and sipped his wine until there was no more waiting within the decanter.

She stopped singing and put aside the instrument.

"I am afraid to stay here alone," she said, "until my kinsmen return. Will you remain with me this night?"

"There is only one answer that I am capable of giving."

She stood then and crossed to his side, touching his cheek with her fingertips. He smiled and touched her chin.

"You are partly of the Elvish kind," she said.

"Yes, I am."

"Dilvish, Dilvish, Dilvish . . ." she said. "The name sounds familiar . . . I know! You are named after the hero of *The Ballad of Portaroy*."

"Yes."

"A goodly tune. Perhaps I'll sing it for you," she said. "Later."

"No," said Dilvish, "it is not one of my favorites."

Then he drew her face to his and kised her lips.

"The fire burns low."

"Yes," he said.

"The room will grow cold."

" 'Tis true."

"Then remove thy green boots, for they are pleasing to the eye but would be awkward in bed."

Dilvish removed his boots, stood, and took her in his arms.

"How came you by these cuts on your cheek?"

"My enemy smote me about the head."

"It would appear he had claws."

"He did."

"An animal?"

"No."

"I will kiss them," she said, "to draw the sting."

Her lips lingered upon his cheek. He crushed her to him then, and she sighed.

"You are strong . . ." she said, and the fire burned low. After a time, it went out.

How long he had slept, he did not know.

There was a sound of splintering wood, and a voice cried out in the night.

He shook his head and stared into her opened eyes.

A strange warmth lay upon his throat. He touched it and his hand became moist.

He shook his head again.

"Please do not be angry," she said. "Remember that I fed you, that I have given you pleasure . . ."

"Vampire . . ." he whispered.

"I would not take your life's blood, Dilvish. Just a drink, just a drink was all I wanted."

There came another blow on the door, as of a battering ram.

He sat up slowly and held his head in his hands.

"Quite a sip," he said. "I think someone's at the door . . ."

"It is my husband," she replied, "Lord Morin."

"Oh? I don't believe we've been introduced . . ."

"I thought he would sleep this night, as he has these many nights past. He fed well a week ago and was sated. But he is like the tiger of the seas. Your blood summoned him."

"I find my position somewhat awkward, Merytha," Dilvish observed, "being guest to a vampire lord I've cuckolded. I don't quite know what one says on these occasions."

"There is nothing to say," she replied. "I hate him. He made me what I am. The only thing I regret is that he was awakened. He means to kill you."

Dilvish rubbed his eyes and reached for his boots.

"What will you do, Dilvish?"

"Apologize, and defend myself."

Three more blows loosened the door upon its hinges.

"Let me in, Merytha!" came a deep voice from without.

"I would that you could kill him and remain with me."

"Vampire," he said.

"I would that you were my lord," she said. "I would be good to you. I am sorry that he was awakened . . . I do not want you to die. Oh, kill him for me! Remain here and love me! You could have slain him, had he not awakened . . . I am not like those in the stories who want your blood. It is good, so good, your blood! And warm! I taste . . . Oh, kill him! Love me!"

The door collapsed, and through the half light Dilvish saw a form round the corner.

Two yellow eyes flickered high above a spade beard, and all the rest of the face was darkness. Morin was as tall as Dilvish and enormously broad of shoulder. He bore a short axe in his right hand.

Dilvish hurled the wine decanter and threw a chair at him.

The decanter missed, and the axe shattered the chair.

Dilvish drew the blade of Selar and guarded himself.

Morin rushed forward and screamed as the point of the invisible blade entered his shoulder.

"What sorcery?" he cried, taking the axe into his left hand.

"I apologize, good sir," said Dilvish, "for abusing custom within your halls. I did not know the lady was wed."

Morin snarled and swung the axe. Dilvish backed away and slashed at his left arm.

"My blood you may not have," he stated. "But I repeat my apology."

"Fool!" cried Morin.

Dilvish parried another axe stroke. In the east, the sky began to lighten. Merytha was crying softly.

Morin crashed into him and locked his arm to his side. Dilvish seized his wrist and they wrestled.

Morin dropped his axe and struck Dilvish in the face. He fell backward, striking his head on the wall.

As the other lunged toward him, Dilvish raised the point of his blade.

Morin uttered a shriek and collapsed, clutching his stomach.

Dilvish wrenched free his blade and stared down at the man, panting.

"You know not what you have done," said Morin.

Merytha rushed toward him where he lay, and he pushed her away.

"Keep her from me!" he said. "Let her not have my blood!"

42

"What mean you?" said Dilvish.

"I knew not what she was when I wedded her," said Morin, "and when I learned, I loved her still. It was not in me to harm her. My servants left me and my castle fell into disrepair, but I could not do what should have been done. Instead I have been her jailer. I forgive you, Elfboot, for she has deceived you. I was drugged. . . . You look to be a strong man, you've proven you are. . . . I hope you are strong enough to do it."

Dilvish turned his head away from the sight and looked at Merytha, where she stood with her back against the bedpost.

"You lied to me," he said. "Vampire!"

"You've done it," she said. "You slew him! My jailer is dead!"

"Yes."

"Will you stay with me now?"

"No," said Dilvish.

"You must," she said. "I want you."

"That," said Dilvish. "I do believe."

"No, not that way. No, I want you to be my lord. All my life I have wanted one with your strength and your strange eyes," she said, " 'in earthly flesh and blood.' Have I not been good to you?"

"I killed this man because of you. I would that I had not."

She shielded her eyes.

"Please stay!" she said. "My life would be empty if you did not. . . . I must retire soon, to a dark, quiet place. Please!" She began to draw heavy breaths. "Please say that you will be here when I awaken tomorrow night."

Dilvish shook his head, slowly.

The room grew lighter.

Her pale eyes widened beneath her sheltering hand.

"You," she said, "you do not mean to harm me, do you?"

Again he shook his head.

"I have done enough harm this night. I must go,

43

Merytha. There is but one cure for your condition and I cannot administer it. Good-bye."

"Do not go," she said. "I will sing to you. I will prepare fine meals. I will love you. I only want a little taste, sometimes, when . . ."

"Vampire," he said.

He heard her footsteps behind him on the stair.

A gray day was dawning about him when he entered the courtyard and placed his hand upon Black's neck.

He heard her gasping as he mounted.

"Do not go . . ." she said. "I love you."

The sun rose as he moved toward the opened gate.

He heard her shriek behind him.

He did not look back.

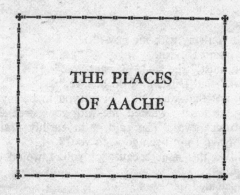

THE PLACES
OF AACHE

As Dilvish the Damned traveled through the North Countries, he passed one day along a twisting road through a low pine-filled valley. His great black mount seemed tireless, but there came a time when Dilvish halted to unpack rations and make a meal. His green boots soundless upon the needles, he spread his cloak and placed his fare upon it.

"There is someone coming."

"Thanks."

He loosened his blade and began to eat standing. Shortly, a large, bearded man on a roan stallion rounded a bend and slowed.

"Ho! Traveler!" the man hailed. "May I join you?"

"You may."

The man halted and dismounted. As he approached, he smiled.

"Rogis is the name," he stated. "And yours?"

"Dilvish."

"You've traveled far?"

"Yes, from the southeast."

"Do you also make a pilgrimage to the shrine?"

"What shrine?"

"That of the goddess Aache, up yonder hill." He gestured up the trail.

"No, I was not even aware of its existence. What is its virtue?"

"The goddess may absolve a man of murder."

"Oh? And you are making pilgrimage for this reason?"

"Yes. I have done it often."

"Do you come from afar?"

"No, I live just up the road. It makes life a lot easier."

"I think I begin to get the picture."

"Good. If you will be so kind as to pass me your purse, you will save the goddess the work involved in an extra absolution."

"Come and take it," Dilvish said, and he smiled.

Rogis's eyes narrowed.

"Not many men have said that to me."

"And I may well be the last."

"Hmm. I'm bigger than you are."

"I've noticed."

"You are making things difficult. Would you be willing to show me whether you're carrying enough coin to make it worth either of our efforts?"

"I think not."

"How about this, then? We split your money, and neither of us takes a bloody chance?"

"No."

Rogis sighed.

"Now the situation has grown awkward. Let me see,

45

are you an archer? No. No bow. No throwing spears either. It would seem that I could ride away without being shot down."

"To ambush me later? I'm afraid I can't permit it. It has become a matter of future self-defense."

"Pity," Rogis said, "but I'll chance it anyway."

He turned back toward his mount, then whirled, his blade in his hand. But Dilvish's own weapon was already drawn, and he parried it and swung a return blow. Rogis cursed, parried, and swung. This went on for six passes, and then Dilvish's blade pierced his abdomen.

A look of surprise crossed his face and he dropped his own weapon to clutch at the one that held him. Dilvish wrenched it free and watched him fall.

"An unlucky day for both of us," Rogis muttered.

"More so for yourself, I'd say."

"You'll not escape this so easily, you know—I'm favored of the goddess—"

"She has peculiar tastes in favorites then."

"I've served her. You'll see . . ." and then his eyes clouded over and he slumped, moaning.

"Black, have you ever heard of this goddess?"

"No," replied the metal statue of a horse, "but then there are many things in this realm of which I have heard nothing."

"Then let us be gone from this place."

"What of Rogis?"

"We will leave him at the crossroads as an advertisment that the world is a safer place. I'll untether his horse and let it find its own way home."

That night, many miles farther north, Dilvish's sleep was troubled. He dreamed that the shade of Rogis came and stood beside him in his camp and knelt, smiling, to place his hands upon his throat. He awoke choking, and a ghostly light seemed to fade away at his side.

"Black! Black! Did you see anything?"

There was silence, then: "I was far away" came

the reply from the unmoving statue, "but I see red marks upon your throat. What happened?"

"I dreamed that Rogis was here, that he tried to throttle me." He coughed and spat.

"It was more than a dream," he decided.

"We'll leave this country soon."

"The sooner the better."

After a time he drifted off to sleep again. At some point Rogis was with him once more. This time the attack was very sudden and even more violent. Dilvish awoke swinging, but his blows fell upon empty air. Now he was certain of the light, Rogis's ghostly outline within it.

"Black, awaken," he said. "We must retrace our path, visit that shrine, lay this ghost. A man has to sleep."

"I am ready. We will be there a little after day-break."

Dilvish broke camp and mounted.

The shrine was a low, sprawling wooden building backed against the rust-streaked rock of the hill, near to its top. The morning sunlight fell upon its face, where a rudely carved double door of dark wood stood closed. Dilvish dismounted and tried it. Finding it bolted, he hammered upon it.

After a long delay, the left side of the door opened and a small man with close-set pale eyes looked out. He wore a coarse brown robe.

"Who are you to trouble us at this hour?" the man inquired.

"One who has been wronged by someone who claimed a special status with your goddess. I wish to be released from whatever doom or spell is involved."

"Oh. You are the one. You're early. Come in."

He swung the door wide and Dilvish stepped through. The room was simply furnished with a few benches and a small altar. There was another door to the rear. A vacant sleeping pallet lay disarrayed near one wall beneath a narrow window.

"My name is Task. Have a seat." The man gestured toward the benches.

"I'll stand."

The small man shrugged.

"All right." He walked back to the pallet and began folding the blankets. "You want the curse lifted, to prevent Rogis's ghost from strangling you."

"You do know!"

"Of course. The goddess does not like to have her servants slaughtered."

Dilvish noticed how, with a deft movement, Task secreted a bottle of a rare southern wine within the rolled pallet. He also noted that each time the man hid his hands within his robe another costly ring vanished from his fingers.

"The servants' victims do not much relish being slaughtered either."

"Tsk. Did you come here to blaspheme or to get absolved?"

"I came here to get this damned curse lifted."

"To do that, you must make an offering."

"Of what must it consist?"

"First, all of your money and any precious stones or metals you have with you."

"The goddess is as much of a highway robber as her servants!"

Task smiled.

"All religions have their secular side. The goddess's following is not large in this sparsely populated area, and the donations of the faithful are not always sufficient to meet operating expenses."

"You said 'first'—first you want all my valuables. What's second?"

"Well, it is only fair that the life you have destroyed be replaced by yourself. A year's service on your part will be ample."

"Doing what?"

"Why, collecting tribute from travelers, as Rogis did."

"I refuse," said Dilvish. "Ask something else."

"Nothing else will do. That is your penance."

Dilvish turned on his heel. He began to pace. He halted.

"What's beyond that door?" he asked suddenly, gesturing to the rear of the room.

"That is a sacred precinct, reserved for the elect—"

Dilvish headed toward it.

"You can't go in there!"

He thrust the door open.

"—especially with a sword!"

He stepped inside. Small oil lamps burned. There was straw on the floor, a feeling of dampness and a peculiar odor that he did not recognize; otherwise, the room was empty. A large, heavy door stood slightly ajar to the rear, however, and from behind it he seemed to hear scratching sounds, retreating.

Task was at his side as he moved to the door. He grasped at his arm but could not hold it back. Dilvish pushed it open and looked through.

Nothing. Darkness and a sense of distance. Rock to the side. A cave.

"That is a storage area."

Dilvish took up an oil lamp and entered. As he proceeded, the smell grew stronger, the dampness heavier. Task followed him.

"It is dangerous back here. There are crevasses, chasms. You might slip—"

"Silence! Or I'll throw you down the first one I see!"

Task dropped back several paces.

Dilvish moved cautiously, holding the lamp high. Rounding a rocky shoulder, he beheld a myriad of sparkles. A pool, recently disturbed.

"This is where it came," he said, "whatever it is," and he advanced upon the pool. "I am going to wait for it. Here. I've a feeling it must emerge, sooner or later. What is it?"

"The goddess . . ." Task said softly. "You should really depart. I have just had a message. Your year's sentence has been remitted. Just leave the money."

49

Dilvish laughed.

"Do goddesses bargain?" he asked.

Sometimes, came a voice in his mind. *Leave it at that.*

A chill passed over his limbs.

"Why do you hide yourself?" he said.

It is not given to many mortals to look upon my kind.

"I don't like blackmail, human or supernatural. Supposing I were to roll this boulder into your pool?"

Abruptly, the water stirred. The face of a woman emerged and regarded him. Her eyes were green and very large, her skin extemely pale. Tight ringlets of black hair covered her head like a helmet. Her chin was pointed, and there was something unnatural to the shape of her tongue when she spoke aloud.

"Very well, you see me," she stated. "I've a mind to show you more."

She continued to rise—neck, shoulders, breasts, all pale—and abruptly all human semblance vanished, for below her waist were more long slender limbs than Dilvish could count.

He cried out and his blade came into his hand. He nearly dropped the lamp.

"I mean you no harm," came her faintly lisping voice. "Recall that it was you who sought this audience."

"Aache—what are you?" he asked.

"My kind is old. Let it go at that. You have caused me difficulties."

"Your man tried to kill me."

"I know. Obviously he chose the wrong victim. Pity. I must go hungry."

The blade twitched in Dilvish's hand.

"What do you mean by that?"

"I eat honey."

"Honey?"

"A sweet liquid made by small flying insects in the far south."

"I know what it is, but I do not understand."

"It is my main dietary requirement. I must have it.

50

There are no flowers, no bees this far north. I must send for it. It is expensive to bring it this distance."

"And that is why you rob travelers?"

"I must have the money, to buy it. My servants get it for me."

"Why do they serve you thus?"

"I might say devotion, but let us be honest. With some men, I can control them over a distance."

"As you sent that phantom to me?"

"I cannot control you directly, as I could Rogis. But I can make your slumber bad."

Dilvish shook his head.

"I've a feeling that the farther I get from here, the less this power would affect me."

"Nor are you incorrect. So go. You would never make me a good servant. Keep your money. Leave me."

"Wait. Have you many servants?"

"That is none of your affair."

"No, it isn't. But I'd a thought. There is mineral wealth in this valley, you know."

"I do not know. I do not understand what you refer to."

"I was involved in several mining operations years ago. When I rode through your valley yesterday, I noticed signs of certain mineral deposits. I believe they are sufficiently rich in the dark metal for which metalworkers to the south would pay well. If you have sufficient servants to set up a digging and smelting operation, you may make out a lot better than you have been by robbing passersby."

"You really think so?"

"It should be easy enough to discover, especially if you will lend me some men."

"Why would you do this for me?"

"Perhaps to make this corner of the world a little safer."

"A strange reason. Go back to the shrine. I am summoning servants now and binding them to you. See whether this thing can be done, then come back to see me—alone."

"I will—Aache."

Suddenly she was gone and the pool sparkled. Dilvish turned and met Task's stare. He walked by him without speaking.

In the days that followed, ore was mined, a smelter constructed, and operations begun. Dilvish smiled as he watched the dark metal pour into its bar molds. Aache smiled when he told her of it.

"And there is much there?" she asked.

"A mountain of it. We can have enough for a good wagonload by next week. Then we can step up the process."

He knelt beside the pool. Her fingers emerged, tentatively touched his hand. When he did not flinch, she reached up and stroked his cheek.

"I could almost wish you were one of my kind," she said, and then she was gone again.

"It has been long since this area was warm and could have had flowers and bees," Black said. "She must be very old."

"It is impossible to tell," Dilvish answered, as they paced the hilltop and looked down into the valley to where the smoke rose. "But if honey is all it takes to make her an honest creature, it's worth this small delay."

"She wants you to take a load south next week?"

"Yes."

"And after that?"

"Her servants should be able to run things from then on."

"As slaves?"

"No, she'll be able to afford to pay them once this gets going."

"I see. One thing . . ."

"Yes?"

"Do not trust that priest Task."

"I don't. He has expensive tastes. I believe he has been pocketing part of the . . . income."

"Of this I know nothing. I spoke, seeing him as one who fears that he may be replaced."

"I will ease his mind on that count soon with my retirement."

The morning of his departure was bright, with only a few snow flurries melting as they descended. The men had sung as they had loaded the wagon the evening before. Now they stood about, baring grins from which their breath puffed cheerily as they clapped him on the shoulder and back, loaded him down with provisions, and saw him on his creaking way.

"I do not appreciate draft duty," Black commented, as soon as they were out of earshot of the camp.

"I'll make it up to you one day."

"I doubt it, but I'll remember it."

No brigands accosted them, for now these forests were clean of them. They made better time when they emerged from the chain of valleys, and by afternoon they had traveled several leagues. Dilvish ate as he rode and Black moved on at a steady pace.

Along toward evening, they heard the sounds of a rider approaching from the rear. They came to a halt when they recognized Task mounted upon Rogis's roan. The horse was in a lather and blowing heavily. It reeled as Task reined in beside the wagon.

"What is the matter?" Dilvish inquired.

"Gone. Dead. Cinders," he said.

"Talk sense!"

"The shrine is burned to the ground. One of the lamps—the straw—"

"What of Aache?"

"She was trapped in the back room—couldn't open the door . . ."

"Dead?"

"Dead."

"Why do you come fleeing?"

"I had to catch you, to discuss my share of the operation."

"I see."

Dilvish saw that he was wearing all of his rings.

"We'd best camp now. Your horse can't go any farther."

"Very well. That field?"

"It will do."

That night Dilvish dreamed a strange dream in which he held a woman tightly, caressing her almost brutally, fearing to look down. He was awakened by a cry of terror.

Sitting up, he beheld a ghostly glow above the form of the man Task. It was already fading, but he would never forget its outline.

"Aache . . . ?"

Sleep, my only friend, my dear friend, came the words from somewhere. *I have but come for that which is mine. It is not so sweet as honey, but it will have to do . . . .*

He covered over the remains of the priest without looking at him. He departed the following morning. He rode the entire day in silence.

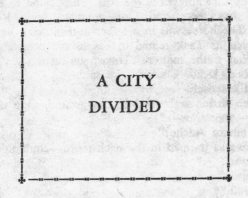

A CITY
DIVIDED

SPRING was twisting its way slowly into the North Country, advancing and retreating by turns, retaining each day something of its gains. Snow still lay heavy upon all the higher peaks, but during the day it melted in the lower regions and the fields lay damp, the streams swelled and raced. Some new green was already evident in the valleys, and on cloudless days such as this the sun dried the trails and the air was warmed to the point of comfort by midday. The traveler on the strange dark horse, but lately up from redelivered Portaroy after the laying of his ghost legions, halted on a rocky rise and gestured to the north.

"Black," he said. "That hill—about half a league off. Did you see something peculiar atop it a moment ago?"

His mount turned its metallic head and stared.

"No. Nor do I now. What did it seem?"

"The outline of some buildings. They're gone now."

"Perhaps it was the sun glinting on the ice."

"Perhaps."

They moved ahead, descending the slope and continuing on their way. On the next hill they mounted, minutes later, they paused again and looked in that direction.

"There!" said the rider who seldom smiled, smiling.

Black shook his head.

"I see it now. It looks like the wall of a city . . ."

"A fresh meal may perhaps be had there—and a bath. And a real bed tonight. Come, let us hurry."

"Check your maps, will you? I am curious what the place is called."

"We will learn that soon enough. Come!"

"Humor me, for old times' sake."

The rider paused, then dipped into his travel bag. He fumbled about, then withdrew a small scroll that he uncased, unrolled, and held before him.

"Hmm," he said after a time. Then he unrolled the map and restored it to its container.

"Well? What is the name of the place?"

"Can't tell. It's not shown."

"Aha!"

"You know this will not be the first error we've found in this map. The mapmaker either forgot the

55

place or did not know about it. Or the town is new."

"Dilvish . . . ?"

"Yes?"

"Do I offer you advice often?"

"Frequently."

"Am I often wrong?"

"I could cite instances."

"I don't fancy the notion of spending the night in a place that is here one moment and gone the next."

"Nonsense! It was just the angle, or some trick of the distance."

"I am suspicious—"

"—by nature. I know. And I am hungry. Fresh fish from one of these streams, broiled with herbs . . ."

Black snorted a tiny wisp of smoke and began walking.

"Your stomach is suddenly a big problem."

"There may be girls, too."

"Hmph!"

The trail leading up the hill to the city gate was not wide, and the gate stood open. Dilvish halted before it but was not challenged. He studied the towers and the walls, but he saw no one. He listened. The only sounds were the wind and the birds at his back.

"Go ahead," he said, and Black bore him through the gate.

Streets ran off to the right and the left, turning with the angles of the wall. The way on which he stood ran straight ahead, ending against buildings at what might be a small plaza. All of these streets were cobbled and well-kept. The buildings were mainly of stone and brick—clean, sharp angled. As they continued along the way leading directly ahead, he noted that no refuse stood or flowed in the ditch at his side.

"Quiet place," said Black.

"Yes."

After perhaps a hundred paces, Dilvish drew upon the reins and dismounted. He entered a shop to his left. A moment later he stepped back outside.

"What is it?"

"Nothing. Empty. No merchandise. Not a stick of furniture."

He crossed over the street and entered another building. He emerged shaking his head.

"The same," he said, remounting.

"Shall we go? You know my feelings."

"Let us have a look at that plaza first. There are no signs of violence thus far. It may be a festival day of some sort."

Black's hooves clicked on the cobbles.

"Pretty dead festival, then."

They rode on, glancing up alleyways, along galleries, into courtyards. There was no activity to be seen, there were no people about. At length they entered the plaza. There were vacant stalls on two sides, a small fountain in the middle that was not operating, and a large statue of two fish near one end. Dilvish paused and regarded the ancient sign. The top fish headed to his left, the bottom one to his right. He shrugged.

"You were right about that," he said. "Let us—"

The air shook from the single note of a bell, swinging within a high tower off to his left.

"Strange . . ."

A youth—blond haired and rosy cheeked, wearing a ruffled white shirt and green hose, a short sword, and a large codpiece—stepped out from behind the statue, smiled, and postured with one hand on his hip.

"Strange?" he said. "Yes, it is. But stranger still, the sight you are about to behold, traveler. Regard!"

He gestured, sweepingly, just as the bell tolled again.

Dilvish turned his head and drew a sudden breath. As silently as cats, the buildings had begun moving about the plaza. They circled, they advanced, they retreated. They rearranged themselves, changing positions with one another as if moving in a ludicrous, cyclopean dance. The bell rang again, and again, as Dilvish watched.

57

Finally: "What sorcery is this?" he inquired of the youth.

"Just so," was the reply. "Sorcery indeed—and it is in the process of rearranging the city into the form of a maze about you."

Dilvish shook his head to the accompaniment of another bell note.

"I am impressed by the display," he said. "But what is its purpose?"

"You might call it a game," said the youth. "When the bell completes its song, several strokes hence, the maze will be laid. You will then have an hour until it strikes again. If you have not found your way out of town and away from here by that time, you will be crushed by the buildings' rearranging themselves once more."

"And why the game?" Dilvish asked, waiting out another tolling before he heard the reply.

"That you will never know, Elfboot, whether you win or lose, for you are only an element of the game. I am also charged to warn you, however, that you may find yourself under attack at various points along whatever route you may choose."

The buildings continued their dance to the sound of the bell.

"I do not care for this game," said Dilvish, drawing his blade, "and I've a mind to play a different one. I have just elected you to guide me out of here. Refuse, and you'll part company with your head."

The youth grinned, and reaching upward with his left hand, he seized a fistful of his own hair while drawing his blade with his right. Brandishing the weapon on high, he brought it down in a fast, hard stroke against the side of his neck. It passed through.

His left hand rose, holding his severed head—still grinning—high above his shoulders. The bell tolled again. The lips moved.

"Did you believe you dealt with mortals, stranger?"

Dilvish frowned.

"I see," he said. "Very well. Deal with him, Black."

58

"Gladly," Black replied, and flames danced within his mouth and filled his eye sockets as he reared in time with another bell stroke.

The face on the severed head showed a look of sudden surprise as an electrical quality came into the air between them. Black's hooves lashed out, crossing in an unhorselike movement as he fell forward, striking the figure to the accompaniment of a sulfurous thunderclap that drowned out the next note of the bell. A scream escaped from the being before them as it vanished in a rush of fire.

The bell tolled twice again as Black recovered his footing and they stood regarding the charred cobbles. Then there was silence. The buildings had ceased their movements.

"All right," Dilvish said at last. "You told me so. Thanks for your action."

Black moved in a circle then, and they regarded the new arrangement of streets that led from the plaza.

"Any preferences?" Black inquired.

"Let's try that one," said Dilvish, gesturing up a sideway to the left.

"All right," said Black. "By the way, I've seen that trick done better."

"Really?"

"I'll tell you about it another time."

They headed up the cobbled way. Nothing moved about them.

The street was narrow and short. Buildings crowded them at either hand. There was an abrupt turn to the right, then to the left again.

"Sst! Over here!" came a voice from their left.

"The first ambush," muttered Dilvish, turning his head and drawing his blade.

A small, dark-eyed man with a pleasant smile, his long gray hair tied into a topknot, his hands raised to shoulder level, empty palms facing outward, watched them from within a doorway. He had on well-worn gray garments.

"It's all right," he whispered sharply. "No trick. I want to help you."

Dilvish did not lower his blade.

"Who are you?" he asked.

"The other side," came the reply.

"What do you mean?"

"This is a game, whether you like it or not," the small man said. "It is between two players. The other side wants you to die in here. Mine only wins if you escape. The other side is responsible for the city. I am responsible for outwitting it."

"How do I know whether you are telling the truth? How can I tell which side is which?"

The man glanced down at his shirtfront and frowned.

"May I lower one hand?"

"Go ahead."

He dropped his right hand and smoothed the baggy garment over his breast. This exposed the emblem of a fish, swimming toward his right. He pointed to it.

"He of the fish that swims to the right," he said, "is the one who wants you out of here safe. Now test my words. Two more turnings, and you had better look for an attack from above."

At this the man leaned backward against the door and it gave way. He closed it behind him, and Dilvish heard the bar drop.

"Let's go," he said to Black.

There were no sounds other than those of Black's hooves as they made the first turn. Dilvish rode with drawn blade, eyes searching every opening.

The second turning led through an archway. He slowed and studied it before continuing on. They passed beneath it and started up the narrow street. They passed a latticed door letting upon a small court-yard. Dilvish looked low as well as high but saw nothing.

Then he heard the sound of metal grating upon stone somewhere overhead. As he glanced upward, he cried, "Back! Back!"

His mount reversed motion without turning, moving

quickly, as a cataract of steaming oil descended and struck the stones before them. Dilvish only glimpsed the figures on the rooftop to his right.

There came a terrific crash that echoed and reverberated about them. Looking back, Dilvish saw that a massive barred gate had been dropped from within the archway. The pool of bubbling oil continued to flow, spreading toward them.

"I won't be able to keep my footing on that," Black said.

"That door, to the right! Break through!"

Black wheeled and crashed against the latticed door. It fell apart, and they were through it and into a small flagged courtyard, a tiny dry fountain at its center, another wooden door at its farther end.

"You cheated!" came a voice from above and to his left. "Were you warned?"

Dilvish looked up.

There, on a small third-floor balcony, stood a man very similar in appearance to their informant, save that his hair was bound back with a blue head strap and on his shirtfront was the emblem of a fish swimming to his left. In his hands he bore a crossbow, which he raised then and sighted.

Dilvish slid down from Black to his right and crouched. He heard the quarrel strike upon Black's metallic hide.

"Through the other gate before he can set it again! I'll follow you!"

Black rushed ahead, not even slowing as he hit the gate. Dilvish sprinted after.

"Cheating! Cheating!" came the cry from behind him.

The street beyond ran in both directions.   .

"To the right," said Dilvish, mounting.

Black hurried off in that direction. They came to a fork. They took the left-hand way, which ran slightly uphill.

"It might be worth risking a climb to the top of a high building," said Dilvish. "I may be able to see the way out."

"Not necessary," came a familiar voice from his right. "I can save you the time and the effort. You've already found one shortcut—back there. It is not very far now."

Dilvish looked into the eyes of that first topknotted man, fish emblem facing to his right. He stood behind a low window, only an arm's distance away.

"But you must hurry. He is already rushing his forces to the gate. If he gets there first, it's all over."

"He could simply have guarded it from the beginning and waited."

"Not permitted. He can't start there. Take the next right, the next left, and two rights. You will come through an alleyway into a wide courtyard. The gate will be on your left and open. Hurry!"

Dilvish nodded and Black raced off, swinging to the right at the next corner.

"Do you believe him?" Black asked.

Dilvish shrugged.

"I must either try it or take a terrible chance."

"What do you mean?"

"Use of the strongest magic I know."

"One of the Awful Sayings you learned in Hell, against the day you meet your enemy?"

"Aye. There's one of the twelve to level a city."

Black turned left, cautiously, then proceeded on.

"How do you think it would fare against a sorcerous construct such as this?"

"For raw power, it is unequaled by earthly magics—"

"But there are no warnings. You never get a second chance if you make a mistake."

"I need not be told."

Black halted at the next corner, peered about it, continued.

"If he was telling the truth, we're almost there," he whispered. "Let us hope we have beaten the other player. And the next time, put more trust in your maps!"

"Aye. Here's the turn. Carefully now . . ."

They rounded the next corner. There was a long alleyway with light at its far end.

"So far it looks as if he spoke true," Black whispered, slowing to soften the sound of his hooves.

He halted as they neared the alley's end, and they looked out upon a courtyard.

The man they had left on the balcony stood in the middle of the yard, smiling in their direction. In his right hand he held a pikestaff.

"You pressed me hard," he said. "But my way was shorter—as you can see."

He looked to his right.

"There is the gate."

He raised his staff and struck it three times upon the ground. Immediately the flagstones about him were raised like trapdoors and figures rose up from out of the ground beneath them. There were perhaps two-score men there. Each bore a pikestaff. Each reached across with his left hand, grasped his hair, and raised his head from his shoulders. All of them laughed then, as they replaced their heads, gripped their pikes with both hands, and started forward across the yard.

"Back!" said Dilvish. "We'd never make it!"

They fled up the alley and turned to the left. They heard the pikemen enter it behind them.

"Other streets opened upon that yard," said Dilvish. "Perhaps we can circle."

"Another street . . ."

"Go left!"

They turned.

"Another."

"Right!"

The way opened upon a square at a crossroads, a fountain at its center. Pikemen suddenly entered from the left and from directly ahead. From behind there still came the sounds of pursuit.

They bore to the right, took another right after a short distance. Farther up the street, a gate fell into place before them. They turned left into a long, arcaded area skirting a garden.

"Cut across the garden!" came a voice from behind a row of shrubs. "There's a gate over there!" The other small man stood, pointing. "Then remember, two lefts and a right, two lefts and a right—all the way around!"

Black's hooves tore through the garden as they headed for the gate. Then he reared and came to a standstill, as the note of a single bell stroke vibrated through the air.

"Oh, oh," said the small man with the topknot.

A building on the left rotated ninety degrees, backed up, and slid off down the street. A stone railing shot away. A tower edged forward. The second small man entered the area and stood beside the other. He was smiling. The first was not.

"Is this it?" Black asked, as an outhouse shot by, passing beneath an arch that was striding toward them.

"I'm afraid so," said Dilvish, straightening and raising both arms over his head. *"Mabra, brahoring Mabra . . ."*

A great wind came down, and within it was a wailing. It spun about without touching them with anything but a chill, and a smoky haze sprang forth from each building.

As Dilvish continued to speak, sounds of cracking and splintering began, followed shortly by the crashes of falling masonry. Somewhere a bell tower tottered and plunged, a final raucous booming emerging from its bell as it descended to shatter upon a rushing shop or residence.

The ground shook as the wailing rose to an ear-splitting howl. The buildings faded within their cloaks of mist. Then came a crack like a hundred lightning-riven trees, and the wind died as suddenly as it had risen.

Dilvish and Black stood upon a sun-swept hilltop. No trace of the city remained about them.

"Congratulations," said Black. "That was very well done."

"To which I must add my own" came a familiar voice from behind them.

Turning, Dilvish saw the small man with the topknot, whose fish swam to his right.

"My deepest apologies," he went on. "I'd no idea we had trapped a brother sorcerer here. That was an Awful Saying, wasn't it? I've never seen one done before."

"Yes, it was."

"Good thing I got close to the protected area in a hurry. My brother, of course, had to go with his city. I want to thank you for that—very much."

"I'd like an explanation now," said Dilvish, "as to what was going on. Had you no better ways to amuse yourselves?"

"Ah, good sir!" said the small man, wringing his hands. "Had you not guessed from the resemblance? We were twins—a most unfortunate situation when both are practitioners of the subtler arts. The power is divided. Each is only half as strong as he might be, if—"

"I begin to see," said Dilvish, "somewhat."

"Yes. We'd tried duels, but we were too evenly matched. So, rather than share a weakness, we had an arrangement. One of us would spend ten years exiled to an astral limbo while the other enjoyed full potency here. At the end of that time, we would play the game to see who would enjoy the next ten years on earth. One of us would erect the city, the other would back the champion to try its maze. I was rather depressed when I drew the champion this time, for the city usually won. But you have been my good fortune, sir. We should have suspected something when we beheld your mount. But who could have guessed an Awful Saying! It must have been hell to learn."

"It was."

"I am of course in your debt, and at full power—almost—now. Is there any way in which I might serve you?"

"Yes," said Dilvish.

65

"Name it."

"I am seeking a man—no, a sorcerer. If you have knowledge of his whereabouts, I want it. To name him here is risky, for his attention might have been drawn to these recent workings of power. His strengths are of the highest, and the darkest. Do you know of whom I speak?"

"I—I am not certain."

Dilvish sighed.

"Very well."

He dismounted, and with the tip of his blade he scratched the name *Jelerak* in the dirt.

The small sorcerer blanched and wrung his hands again.

"Oh, good sir! You seek your death!"

"No. His," Dilvish said, rubbing out the name with his toe. "Can you help me?"

The other swallowed.

"He has seven castles that I know of in different parts of the world. All are defended differently. He employs servants both human and unnatural. It is said that he has ways of transporting himself quickly among these keeps. How is it that you do not know these things?"

"I have been away for a long while. Bear with me. Where are they located?"

"I believe I may know who you are," said the sorcerer, kneeling and drawing in the earth with his finger.

Dilvish crouched beside him and watched the map take shape.

". . . Here is the one at the edge of the world, which I have seen only in visions. Here is the Red Keep. . . . Another lies to the far south . . ."

Dilvish inscribed them in his mind as they appeared before him.

". . . Then the nearest seems to be this one you call the Tower of Ice," Dilvish said, "over a hundred leagues to the north and west of here. I had heard rumor of such a place. I had been seeking it."

"Take counsel of me, Deliverer," he said, rising. "Do not—"

The city stood all around them again, but changed, beginning lower and sweeping down the hillside for as far as the eye could see.

"You didn't—uh—summon it back for a small joke, did you?" the sorcerer asked.

"No."

"I was afraid you'd say that. Came up awfully quiet, didn't it?"

"Yes."

"A lot bigger than Stradd and I could ever make them, too. What now? Do you think he wants to run us through it?"

A dark mass occurred in the sky overhead.

"I'd do it gladly, if he would await me within."

"Don't say that, friend! Look!"

Like slow lightning, sheets of fire descended from the heavens, silently, falling upon the new city about them. In moments it began to blaze. They smelled the smoke. Ashes drifted by. Soon they were ringed by a giant wall of flame, and waves of heat fell upon them.

"That is very nicely done," observed the sorcerer, mopping his brow with his sleeve. "I am going to give you my name—Strodd—as an act of extreme generosity on my part, since we may be under sentence of death, anyway—and I believe I've already guessed yours. Right?"

"I'd say."

The fires began to subside. There was no city beneath them.

"Yes, that *is* nicely done," Strodd remarked. "I believe the demonstration is about over, but I wonder why he didn't simply divert it upon us?"

Black laughed—a harsh, metallic thing.

"There are reasons," he said.

The fire flickered and vanished, leaving the sunny hilltop exactly as it had been but a while before.

"Well, there you are," Strodd said. "I am suddenly anxious to undertake a long journey, for my health.

One grows somewhat attenuated wandering about in astral limbos. I still owe you something, but I am afraid of the company you might be keeping. I would rather you called on me for several small matters rather than the big one I fear you might be headed for—if you know what I mean?"

"I'll remember," said Dilvish, smiling, and he mounted Black and turned his head toward the northwest.

Strodd winced.

"I was afraid you'd be going that way," he said. "Well, good luck to you anyhow."

"And yourself."

Dilvish tossed the man a small salute before he rode off.

"The Tower of Ice?" said Black.

"The Tower of Ice."

When Dilvish looked back, the hilltop was empty.

THE WHITE BEAST

ALL that day, as he crossed the ice field, the rider of the burnished black beast had known that he was pursued. He had glimpsed the great loping white form far back among the drifts. Now, with moonlight sparkling upon the sleek and snowy forms and an icy wind sweeping down from the mountains and across the nighted plain, he heard the first howl of his pursuer.

But the mountains themselves lay very near now. Somewhere at their base, perhaps, a hollow, a cave, a fortified shelter—a place where he might rest with rock at his back and beside him, a fire before him, his blade across his knees.

The howling came again. His great black mount moved more quickly. Large boulders lay strewn ahead of them, beside them now . . . He moved among them, his eyes searching the ice-coated talus for signs of an opening—anywhere.

"There, up ahead" came the low voice from below and before him, as the beast spoke.

"Yes, I see it. Can we fit?"

"If not, I'll enlarge it. It is dangerous to seek further. There may be no other."

"True."

They halted before the opening. The man dismounted, his green boots soundless on the snow. His black, horselike mount entered first.

"It is larger than it looks, empty and dry. Come in."

The man entered the cave, dipping his head below its outer rim. He dropped to his knees and felt for tinder.

"A few sticks, a branch, leaves . . ."

He heaped them and seated himself. The beast remained standing at his back. He unclasped his blade and placed it near to hand.

There came another howl, much nearer.

"I wish that damned white wolf would get up his courage to attack. I won't be able to sleep till we've settled our differences," said the man, locating his flint. "All day it's circled and trailed, watching, waiting . . ."

"I believe it is me that it fears most," said the dark form. "It senses that I am unnatural, and that I will protect you."

"I would fear you, too," said the man, laughing.

"But yours is a human intelligence. What of its?"

"What do you imply?"

"Nothing. Really. I don't know. Eat. Rest. I will guard you."

The leaves took fire beneath showers of sparks, smouldered.

"If it were to brave the flame, spring quickly, and seize me, it might drag me out there—to some snowy crust where one of your bulk would flounder. That is how I would do it."

"Now you are crediting it with too much wisdom."

The man fed the fire, unwrapped his rations.

"I see it moving, among the rocks. It is hungry, but it thinks to wait—for the right moment."

He unsheathed his blade.

"Is there any special way to tell a were-beast?" he asked.

"Not unless you see it changing, or hear it speaking."

"Hello out there!" the man called suddenly. "Make a deal? I'll share my rations with you, then wave good-bye. All right?"

Only the wind made answer.

He took up a piece of meat, skewered it, and warmed it. He cut it in half then and set a piece of it to one side.

"You are being more than a little ridiculous," said his companion.

The man shrugged and began eating. He melted snow for water, mixed some wine with it, drank.

An hour passed. He sat wrapped in his cloak and a folded blanket, feeding the remaining sticks to the fire. Outside the snowy shape moved nearer. He caught the glint of his firelight on its eyes for the first time, from off to the left and at a point not visible to his dark companion. He said nothing. He watched. The eyes drifted nearer—large, yellow.

Finally they settled, low, just around the corner of the cave mouth.

"The meat!" came a panted whisper.

He placed a hand upon the foreleg of his companion, signaling it to stillness. With his other hand, he picked up the piece of meat and tossed it outside. It vanished immediately, and he heard the sounds of chewing.

"That is all?" came the voice, after a time.

"Half of my own ration, as I promised," he whispered.

"I am very hungry. I fear I must eat you also. I am sorry."

"I know that. And I, too, am sorry, but what I have left must feed me until I reach the Tower of Ice. Also, I must destroy you if you attempt to take me."

"The Tower of Ice? You will die there and the food be wasted, your own body-meat be wasted. The master of that place will kill you. Did you not know?"

"Not if I kill him first."

The white beast panted for a time. Then: "I am so hungry," it said again. "Soon I must try to take you. Some things are worse than death."

"I know that."

"Would you tell me your name?"

"Dilvish."

"It seems I heard that name once, long ago . . ."

"Perhaps."

"If he does not kill you— Look at me! I, too, once tried to kill him. I, too, was once a man."

"I do not know the spell which might unbind you."

"Too late. I care no more for that. Only for food."

There came a slobbering sound, followed by a sharp intake of breath. The man took his blade into his hand and waited.

Then: "I remember hearing of a Dilvish long ago, called the Deliverer" came the slow words. "He was strong."

Silence.

"I am he."

Silence.

"Let me move a little nearer. . . . And your boots are green!"

The white form withdrew again. The yellow eyes met his own and stared.

"I am hungry, always hungry."

"I know."

"I know of only one thing that is stronger. You know that, too. Good-bye."

71

"Good-bye."

The eyes turned away. The shadow form was gone from beside the cave. Later Dilvish heard a howling in the distance. Then silence.

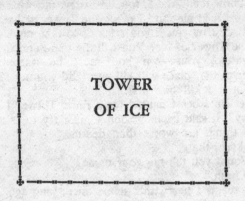

TOWER
OF ICE

THE dark, horse-shaped beast paused on the icy trail. Head turned to the left and upward, it regarded the castle atop the glistening mountain, as did its rider.

"No," the man finally stated.

The black beast continued on, ice cracking beneath its cloven metal hooves, snow blowing about it.

"I'm beginning to suspect that there is no trail," the beast announced after a time. "We've come more than halfway around."

"I know," replied the muffled, green-booted rider. "I might be able to scale the thing, but that would mean leaving you behind."

"Risky," his mount replied. "You know my value in certain situations—especially the one you court."

"True. But if it should prove the only way . . ."

They moved on for some time, pausing periodically to study the prominence.

"Dilvish, there was a gentler part of the slope—some distance back," the beast announced. "If I'd a good start, I could bear you quite a distance up it. Not all of the way to the top, but near."

72

"If that should prove the only way, Black, we'll go that route," the rider replied, breath steaming before him to be whipped away by the wind. "We might as well check further first, though. Hello! What is—"

A dark form came hurtling down the side of the mountain. When it seemed that it was about to strike the ice before them, it spread pale-green, batlike wings and pulled itself aloft. It circled quickly, gaining altitude, then dove toward them.

Immediately his blade was in his hand, held vertically before him. Dilvish leaned back, eyes on the approaching creature. At the sight of his weapon, it veered off, to return immediately. He swung at it and missed. It darted away again.

"Obviously our presence is no longer a secret," Black commented, turning so as to face the flying thing.

The creature dove once more and Dilvish swung again. It turned at the last moment, to be struck by the side of his blade. It fell then, fluttered, rose into the air again, circled several times, climbed higher, turned away. It began to fly back up along the side of the Tower of Ice.

"Yes, it would seem we have lost the advantage of surprise," Dilvish observed. "Actually, I'd thought he would have noted us sooner."

He sheathed his blade.

"Let's go find that trail—if there is one."

They continued on their way about the base of the mountain.

Corpselike, the green and white face stared out of the mirror. No one stood before it to cast such an image. The high stone hall was reflected behind it, threadbare tapestries on its walls, several narrow windows, the long, heavy dining table, a candelabrum flickering at its farther end. The wind made moaning noises down a nearby chimney, alternately flattening and drawing the flames in the wide fireplace.

The face seemed to be regarding the diners: a thin, dark-haired, dark-eyed young man in a black doublet lined with green, who toyed with his food and whose

73

nervous gestures carried his fingers time and again to the heavy, black metal ring with the pale pink stone that depended from a chain about his neck; and a girl, whose hair and eyes matched the man's, whose generous mouth quirked into occasional odd, quick smiles as she ate with better appetite. She had a brown and red cloak thrown about her shoulders, its ends folded across her lap. Her eyes were not so deep-set as the man's and they did not dart as his did.

The thing in the mirror moved its pale lips.

"The time is coming," it announced, in a deep, expressionless voice.

The man leaned forward and cut a piece of meat. The girl raised her wineglass. Something seemed to flutter against one of the windows for a moment.

From somewhere far up the long corridor to the girl's right, an agonized voice rang out:

"Release me! Oh, please don't do this! Please! It hurts so much!"

The girl sipped her wine.

"The time is coming," the thing in the mirror repeated.

"Ridley, would you pass the bread?" the girl asked.

"Here."

"Thank you."

She broke off a piece and dipped it into the gravy. The man watched her eat, as if fascinated by the act.

"The time is coming," the thing said again.

Suddenly Ridley slapped the table. His cutlery rattled. Beads of wine fell across his plate.

"Reena, can't you shut that damned thing off?" he asked.

"Why, you summoned it," she said sweetly. "Can't you just wave your wand or snap your fingers and give it the proper words?"

He slapped the table again, half rising from his seat.

"I will not be mocked!" he said. "Shut it off!"

She shook her head slowly.

"Not my sort of magic," she replied, less sweetly. "I don't fool with things like that."

From up the hall came more cries:

"It hurts! Oh, please! It hurts so . . ."

". . . Or that," she said more sternly. "Besides, you told me at the time that it was serving a useful purpose."

Ridley lowered himself into his seat.

"I was not—myself," he said softly, taking up his wineglass and draining it.

A mummy-faced individual in dark livery immediately rushed forward from the shadowy corner beside the fireplace to refill his glass.

Faintly, and from a great distance, there came a rattling, as of chains. A shadowy form fluttered against a different window. Ridley fingered his neck chain and drank again.

"The time is coming," announced the corpse-colored face under glass.

Ridley hurled his wineglass at it. It shattered, but the mirror remained intact. Perhaps the faintest of smiles touched the corners of that ghastly mouth. The servant hurried to bring him another glass.

There came more cries from up the hall.

"It's no good," Dilvish stated. "We've more than circled it. I don't see any easy way up."

"You know how sorcerers can be. Especially this one."

"True."

"You should have asked that werewolf you met a while back about it."

"Too late now. If we just keep going, we should come to that slope you mentioned pretty soon, shouldn't we?"

"Eventually," Black replied, trudging on. "I could use a bucket of demon juice. I'd even settle for wine."

"I wish I had some wine here myself. I haven't sighted that flying thing again." He looked up into the darkening sky, to where the snow- and ice-decked castle stood with a high window illuminated. "Unless I've glimpsed it darting about up there," he said. "Hard to tell, with the snow and shadows."

"Strange that he didn't send something a lot more deadly."

"I've thought of that."

They continued on for a long while. The lines of the slope softened as they advanced, the icy wall dipping toward a slightly gentler inclination. Dilvish recognized the area as one they had passed before, though Black's earlier hoof prints had been completely obliterated.

"You're pretty low on supplies, aren't you?" Black asked.

"Yes."

"Then I guess we'd better do something—soon."

Dilvish studied the slope as they moved along its foot.

"It gets a little better, farther ahead," Black remarked. Then: "That sorcerer we met—Strodd—had the right idea."

"What do you mean?"

"He headed south. I hate this cold."

"I didn't realize it bothered you, too."

"It's a lot hotter where I come from."

"Would you rather be back there?"

"Now that you mention it, no."

Several minutes later they rounded an icy mass. Black halted and turned his head.

"That's the route I'd choose—over there. You can judge it best from here."

Dilvish followed the slope upward with his eyes. It reached about three quarters of the way up to the castle. Above it the wall rose sheer and sharp.

"How far up do you think you can get me?" he asked.

"I'll have to stop when it goes vertical. Can you scale the rest?"

Dilvish shaded his eyes and squinted.

"I don't know. It looks bad. But then, so does the grade. Are you sure you can make it that far?"

Black was silent for a time, then: "No, I'm not," he said. "But we've been all the way around, and this is the only place where I think we've got a chance."

Dilvish lowered his eyes.

"What do you say?"

"Let's do it."

"I don't see how you can sit there eating like that!" Ridley declared, throwing down his knife. "It's disgusting!"

"One must keep up one's strength in the face of calamities," Reena replied, taking another mouthful. "Besides, the food is exceptionally good tonight. Which one prepared it?"

"I don't know. I can't tell the staff apart. I just give them orders."

"The time is coming," stated the mirror.

Something fluttered against the window again and stopped, hanging there, a dark outline. Reena sighed, lowered her utensils, rose. She rounded the table and crossed to the window.

"I am not going to open the window in weather like this!" she shouted. "I told you that before! If you want to come in, you can fly down one of the chimneys! Or not, as you please!"

She listened a moment to a rapid chittering noise from beyond the pane.

"No, not just this once!" she said then. "I told you that before you went out in it!"

She turned and stalked back to her seat, her shadow dancing on a tapestry as the candles flickered.

"Oh, don't. . . . Please, don't. . . . Oh!" came a cry from up the hall.

She settled into her chair once more, ate a final mouthful, took another sip of wine.

"We've got to do something," Ridley said, stroking the ring on the chain. "We can't just sit here."

"I'm quite comfortable," she answered.

"You're in this as much as I am."

"Hardly."

"He's not going to look at it that way."

"I wouldn't be too sure."

Ridley snorted.

"Your charms won't save you from the reckoning."

She protruded her lower lip in a mock pout.

"On top of everything else, you insult my femininity."

"You're pushing me, Reena!"

"You know what to do about it, don't you?"

"No!" He slammed his fist against the table. "I won't!"

"The time is coming," said the mirror.

He covered his face with his hands and lowered his head.

"I—I'm afraid . . ." he said softly.

Now out of his sight, a look of concern tightened her brow, narrowed her eyes.

"I'm afraid of—the other," he said.

"Can you think of any other course?"

"You do something! You've got powers!"

"Not on that level," she said. "The other is the only one I can think of who would have a chance."

"But he's untrustworthy! I can't anticipate him anymore!"

"But he gets stronger all the time. Soon he may be strong enough."

"I—I don't know. . . ."

"Who got us into this mess?"

"That's not fair!"

He lowered his hands and raised his head just as a rattling began within the chimney. Particles of soot and mortar fell upon the flames.

"Oh, really!" she said.

"That crazy old bat—" he began, turning his head.

"Now, that isn't nice either," Reena stated. "After all—"

Ashes were scattered as a small body crashed into the flaming logs, bounced away, hopped about the floor flapping long, green, membranous wings, beating sparks from its body fur. It was the size of a small ape, with a shriveled, nearly human face. It squeaked as it hopped, some of its noises sounding strangely like human curses. Finally it came to a stooped standstill, raised its head, turned burning eyes upon them.

"Try to set fire to me!" it chirped shrilly.

"Come on now! Nobody tried to set fire to you." Reena said.

". . . Said 'chimney'!" it cried.

"There are plenty of chimneys up there," Reena stated. "It's pretty stupid to choose a smoking one."

". . . Not stupid!"

"What else can you call it?"

The creature sniffed several times.

"I'm sorry," Reena said. "But you could have been more careful."

"The time is coming," said the mirror.

The creature turned its small head, stuck out its tongue.

". . . Lot you know," it said. "He . . . he beat me!"

"Who? Who beat you?" Ridley asked.

". . . The avenger." It made a sweeping, downward gesture with its right wing. "He's down there."

"Oh, my!" Ridley paled. "You're quite certian?"

". . . He beat me," the creature repeated. Then it began to bounce along the floor, beat at the air with its wings, and flew to the center of the table.

Somewhere, faintly, a chain was rattled.

"How—how do you know he is the avenger?" Ridley asked.

The creature hopped along the table, tore at the bread with its talons, stuffed a piece into its mouth, chewed noisily.

". . . My little ones, my pretty ones," it chanted after a time, glancing about the hall.

"Stop that!" Reena said. "Answer his question! How do you know who it is?"

It raised its wings to its ears.

"Don't shout! Don't shout!" it cried. ". . . I saw! I know! He beat me—poor side!—with a sword!" It paused to hug itself with its wings. ". . . I only went to look up close. My eyes are not so good. . . . He rides a demon beast! Circling, circling—the mountain! Coming, coming—here!"

Ridley shot a look at Reena. She compressed her lips, then shook her head.

"Unless it is airborne it will never make it up the tower," she said. "It wasn't a winged beast, was it?"

". . . No. A horse," the creature replied, tearing at the bread again.

"There was a slide near the south face," Ridley said. "But no. Even so. Not with a horse . . ."

". . . A demon horse."

"Even with a demon horse!"

"The pain! The pain! I can't stand it!" came a shrill cry.

Reena raised her wineglass, saw that it was empty, lowered it again. The mummy-faced man rushed from the shadows to fill it.

For several moments they watched the winged creature eat. Then: "I don't like this," Reena said. "You know how devious he can be."

"I know."

". . . And green boots," chirped the creature. ". . . Elfboots. Always to land on his feet. You burned me, he beat me. . . . Poor Meg! Poor Meg! He'll get you, too . . ."

It hopped down and skittered across the floor.

". . . My little ones, my pretty ones!" it called.

"Not here! Get out of here!" Ridley cried. "Change or go away! Keep them out of here!"

". . . Little ones! Pretties!" came the fading voice as Meg ran up the corridor in the direction of the screams.

Reena swirled the wine in her glass, took a drink, licked her lips.

"The time has come," the mirror suddenly announced.

"Now what are you going to do?" Reena asked.

"I don't feel well," Ridley said.

When they came to the foot of the slope, Black halted and stood like a statue for a long while, studying it. The snow continued to fall. The wind drove the flakes past them.

After several minutes, Black advanced and tested the grade, climbing several paces, standing with his full weight upon it, stamping and digging with his hooves, head lowered.

Finally he backed down the slope and turned away.

"What is the verdict?" Dilvish inquired.

"I am still willing to try. My estimate of our chances is unchanged. Have you given any thought to what you are going to do if—rather, when—you make it to the top?"

"Look for trouble," Dilvish said. "Defend myself at all times. Strike instantly if I see the enemy."

Black began to walk slowly away from the mountain.

"Almost all of your spells are of the offensive variety," Black stated, "and most are too terrible to be used, except in final extremes. You should really take the time to learn some lesser and intermediate ones, you know."

"I know. This is a fine time for a lecture on the state of the art."

"What I am trying to say is that if you get trapped up there, you know how to level the whole damned place and yourself with it. But you don't know how to charm the lock on a door—"

"That is *not* a simple spell!"

"No one said that it was. I am merely pointing out your deficiencies."

"It is a little late for that, isn't it?"

"I am afraid so," Black replied. "So, there are three good general spells of protection against magical attack. You know as well as I do that your enemy can break through any of them. The stronger ones, though, might slow him long enough for you to do something. I can't let you go up there without one of them holding you."

"Then lay the strongest upon me."

"It takes a full day to do it."

Dilvish shook his head.

"In this cold? Too long. What about the others?"

"The first one we may dismiss as insufficient against any decent operator in the arts. The second takes the better part of an hour to call into being. It will give you good protection for about half a day."

Dilvish was silent for a moment. Then: "Let's be about it," he said.

"All right. But even so, there must be servants, to keep the place running. You are probably going to find yourself outnumbered."

Dilvish shrugged.

"It may not be much of a staff," he said, "and there'd be no need to maintain a great guard in an inaccessible spot like this. I'll take my chances."

Black came to the place he deemed sufficiently distant from the slope. He turned and faced the tower.

"Get your rest now," he stated, "while I work your protection. It will probably be the last you have for a while."

Dilvish sighed and leaned forward. Black began speaking in a strange voice. His words seemed to crackle in the icy air.

The latest scream ceased on a weakened note. Ridley got to his feet and moved across the hall to a window. He rubbed at the frosted pane with the palm of his hand, a quick, circular motion. He placed his face near the area he had cleared, holding his breath.

Finally: "What do you see?" Reena asked him.

"Snow," he muttered, "ice . . ."

"Anything else?"

"My reflection," he answered angrily, turning away.

He began to pace. When he passed the face in the mirror, its lips moved.

"The time is come," it said.

He replied with an obscenity. He continued pacing, hands clasped behind his back.

"You think Meg really saw something down there?" he asked.

"Yes. Even the mirror has changed its tune."

"What do you think it is?"

"A man on a strange mount."

"Perhaps he's not actually coming here. Maybe he's on his way someplace else."

She laughed softly.

"Just on his way to the neighborhood tavern for a few drinks," she said.

"All right! All right! I'm not thinking clearly! I'm upset! Supposing—just supposing—he does make it up here. He's only one man."

"With a sword. When was the last time you had one in your hands?"

Ridley licked his lips.

". . . And he must be fairly sturdy," she said, "to have come so far across these wastes."

"There are the servants. They obey me. Since they are already dead he'd have a hard time killing them."

"That would tend to follow. On the other hand, they're a bit slower and clumsier than ordinary folk—and they can be dismembered."

"You don't do much to cheer a man up, you know?"

"I am trying to be realistic. If there is a man out there wearing Elfboots, he has chance of making it up here. If he is of the hardy sort and a decent swordsman, then he has a chance of doing what he was sent to do."

". . . And you'll still be mocking and bitching while he lops off my head? Just remember that yours will roll, too!"

She smiled.

"I am in no way responsible for what happened."

"Do you really think he'll see it that way? Or care?"

She looked away.

"You had a chance," she said slowly, "to be one of the truly great ones. But you wouldn't follow the normal courses of development. You were greedy for power. You rushed things. You took risks. You created a doubly dangerous situation. You could have explained the sealing as an experiment that went bad. You could have apologized. He would have been irritated, but he would have accepted it. Now, though, when you can't undo what you did—or do much of anything else, for that matter—he is going to know what happened. He is going to know that you were trying to multiply your power to the point where you could even challenge him. You know what his response has to be under the circumstances. I can almost sympathize with him. If it were me, I would have to do the same thing—destroy you before you get control of the other. You've become an extremely dangerous man."

"But I am powerless! There isn't a damned thing I can do! Not even shut off that simple mirror!" he cried, gesturing toward the face that had just spoken again. "In this state I'm no threat to anybody!"

"Outside of his being inconvenienced by your having cut off his access to one of his strongholds," she said, "he would have to consider the possibility that you keep drawing back from—namely, that if you gain control of the other, you will be one of the most powerful sorcerers in the world. As his apprentice— pardon me, ex-apprentice—who has just apparently usurped a part of his domain, only one thing can follow—a sorcerous duel in which you will actually have a chance of destroying him. Since such a duel has not yet commenced, he must have guessed that you are not ready—or that you are playing some sort of waiting game. So he has sent a human avenger, rather than run the risk that you've turned this place into some sort of magical trap."

"The whole thing could simply have been an accident. He'd have to consider that possibility, too. . . ."

"Under the circumstances, would *you* take the risk of assuming that and waiting? You know the answer. You'd dispatch an assassin."

"I've been a good servant. I've taken care of this place for him. . . ."

"Be sure to petition him for mercy on that count the next time that you see him."

Ridley halted and wrung his hands.

"Perhaps you could seduce him. You're comely enough . . ."

Reena smiled again.

"I'd lay him on an iceberg and not complain," she said. "If it would get us off the hook, I'd give him the high ride of his long life. But a sorcerer like that—"

"Not him. The avenger."

"Oh."

She blushed suddenly. Then she shook her head.

"I can't believe that anyone who has come all this way could be dissuaded from his purposes by a bit of dalliance, even with someone of my admitted charms. Not to mention the thought of the penalty for his failure. No. You are skirting the real issue again. There is only one way out for you, and you know what that is."

He dropped his eyes, fingered the ring on the chain.

"The other . . ." he said. "If I had control of the other, all of our problems would be over . . ."

He stared at the ring as if hynotized by it.

"That's right," she said. "It's the only real chance."

"But you know what I fear . . ."

"Yes. I fear it, too."

". . . That it may not work—that the other may gain control of *me!*"

"So, either way you are doomed. Just remember, one way it is certain. The other . . . That way there is still a chance."

"Yes," he said, still not looking at her. "But you don't know the horror of it!"

"I can guess."

"But you don't have to go through it!"

"I didn't create the situation either."

He glared at her.

"I'm sick of hearing you protest your innocence just because the other is not your creation! I went to you first and told you everything I proposed to do! Did you try to talk me out of it? No! You saw the gains in store for us! You went along with my doing it!"

She covered her mouth with her fingertips and yawned delicately.

"Brother," she said, "I suppose that you are right. It doesn't change anything, though, does it? Anything that has to be done . . . ?"

He gnashed his teeth and turned away.

"I won't do it. I can't!"

"You may feel differently about it when he comes knocking at your door."

"We have plenty of ways to deal with a single man —even a skilled swordsman!"

"But don't you see? Even if you succeed you are

85

only postponing the decision, not solving the problem."

"I want the time. Maybe I can think of some way
to gain an edge over the other."

Reena's features softened.

"Do you really believe that?"

"Anything is possible, I suppose. . . ."

She sighed and stood. She moved toward him.

"Ridley, you are deceiving yourself," she said.
"You will never be any stronger than you are now."

"Not true!" he cried, beginning to pace again. "Not
true!"

Another scream came from up the hall. The mirror
repeated its message.

"Stop him! We have to stop him! *Then* I'll worry
about the other!"

He turned and tore out of the room. Reena lowered
the hand she had raised toward him and returned to
the table to finish her wine. The fireplace continued
to sigh.

Black completed the spell. They remained motionless for a brief while after that.

Then: "That's it?" Dilvish asked.

"It is. You are now protected through the second
level."

"I don't feel any different."

"That's how you should feel."

"Is there anything special that I should do to in-
voke its defense, should the need arise?"

"No, it is entirely automatic. But do not let that
dissuade you from exercising normal caution about
things magical. Any system has its weak points. But
that was the best I could do in the time that we had."

Dilvish nodded and looked toward the tower of ice.
Black raised his head and faced it, also.

"Then I guess that all of the preliminaries are out
of the way," Dilvish said.

"So it would seem. Are you ready?"

"Yes."

Black began to move forward. Glancing down, Dilvish noted that his hooves seemed larger now, flatter. He wanted to ask about it, but the wind came faster as they gained speed and he decided to save his breath. The snow stung his cheeks, his hands. He squinted and leaned farther forward.

Still running on a level surface, Black's pace increased steadily, one hoof giving an almost bell-like tone as it struck some pebble. Soon they were moving faster than any horse could run. Everything to both sides became a snowy blur. Dilvish tried not to look ahead, to protect his eyes, his face. He clung tightly and thought about the course he had come.

He had escaped from Hell itself, after two centuries' torment. Most of the humans he had known were long dead and the world somewhat changed. Yet the one who had banished him, damning him as he did, remained—the ancient sorcerer Jelerak. In the months since his return, he had sought that one, once the call of an ancient duty had been discharged before the walls of Portaroy. Now, he told himself, he lived but for vengeance. And this, this tower of ice, one of the seven strongholds of Jelerak, was the closest he had yet come to his enemy. From Hell he had brought a collection of Awful Sayings—spells of such deadly potency as to place the speaker in as great a jeopardy as the victim should their rendering be even slightly less than flawless. He had only used one since his return and had been successful in leveling an entire small city with it. His shudder was for the memory of that day on that hilltop, rather than for the icy blasts that now assailed him.

A shift in equilibrium told him that Black had reached the slope and commenced the ascent. The wind was making a roaring sound. His head was bowed and turned against the icy pelting. He could feel the rapid crunching of Black's hooves beneath him, steady, all of the movements extraordinarily powerful. If Black should slip, he knew that it would be all over for him. . . . Good-bye again, world—and Jelerak still unpunished . . .

As the gleaming surface fled by beneath him, he

tried to push all thoughts of Jelerak and death and vengeance from his mind. As he listened to the wind and cracking ice, his thoughts came free of the moment, drifting back over the unhappy years, past the days of his campaigns, his wanderings, coming to rest on a misty morning in the glades of far Elfland as he rode to the hunt near the Castle Mirata. The sun was big and golden, the breezes cool, and everywhere— green. He could almost smell the earth, feel the texture of tree bark. . . . Would he ever know that again, the way he once had?

An inarticulate cry escaped him, hurled against the wind and destiny and the task he had set himself. He cursed then and squeezed harder with his legs as his equilibrium shifted again and he knew that the course had steepened.

Black's hooves pounded perhaps a trifle more slowly. Dilvish's hands and feet and face were growing numb. He wondered how far up they were. He risked a glance forward but saw only rushing snow. We've come a long way, he decided. Where will it end?

He called back his memory of the slope as seen from below, tried to judge their position. Surely they were near the halfway point. Perhaps they had even passed it. . . .

He counted his heartbeats, counted Black's hoof falls. Yes, it did seem that the great beast was slowing. . . .

He chanced another look ahead.

This time he caught the barest glimpse of the towering rise above and before him, sparkling through the evening, sheer, glassy. It obliterated most of the sky now, so he knew that they must be close.

Black continued to slow. The roaring wind lowered its voice. The snow came against him with slightly diminished force.

He looked back over his shoulder. He could see the great slope spread out behind them, glistening like the mosaic tiles in the baths at Ankyra. Down, down and back . . . They *had* come a great distance.

Black slowed even more. Now Dilvish could hear as

well as feel the crunching of crusted snow and ice beneath them. He eased his grip slightly, leaned back a little, raised his head. There was the last stage of the tower, glistening darkly, much nearer now.

Abruptly, the winds ceased. The monolith must be blocking them, he decided. The snow drifted far more gently here. Black's pace had become a canter, though he was laboring no less diligently than before. The journey up the white-smeared tunnel was nearing its end.

Dilvish adjusted his position again, to better study the high escarpment. At this quarter, its surface had resolved itself into a thing of textures. From the play of shadow, he could make out prominences, crevices. Bare rock jutted in numerous places. Quickly he began tracing possible routes to the top.

Black slowed further, almost to a walk, but they now were near to the place where the greatest steepness began. Dilvish cast about for a stopping point.

"What do you think of that ledge off to the right, Black?" he asked.

"Not much" came the reply. "But that's where we're headed. The trickiest part will be making it up onto the shelf. Don't let go yet."

Dilvish clung tightly as Black negotiated a hundred paces, a hundred more.

"It looks wider from here than it did from back there," he observed.

"Yes. Higher, too. Hang on. If we slip here, it's a long way back down."

Black's pace increased slightly as he approached the ledge that stood at nearly the height of a man above the slope. It was indented several span into the cliff face.

Black leapt.

His hind hooves struck a waist-high prominence, a bare wrinkle of icy rock running horizontally below the ledge. His momentum bore him up past it. It cracked and fell away, but by then his forelegs were on the shelf and his rear ones had straightened with a tiny spring. He scrambled up over the ledge and found his footing.

"You all right?" he asked.

"Yes," said Dilvish.

Simultaneously they turned their heads, slowly, and looked back down to where the winds whipped billows of white, like clouds of smoke across the sparkling way. Dilvish reached out and patted Black's shoulder.

"Well done," he said. "Here and there, I was a little worried."

"Did you think you were the only one?"

"No. Can we make it back down again?"

Black nodded.

"We'll have to move a lot more slowly than we did coming up, though. You may even have to walk beside me, holding on. We'll see. This ledge seems to go back a little way. I'll explore it while you are about your business. There may be a slightly better route down. It should be easier to tell from up here."

"All right," Dilvish said, dismounting on the side nearest the cliff face.

He removed his gloves and massaged his hands, blew on them, tucked them into his armpits for a time.

"Have you decided upon the place for your ascent?"

"Off to the left." Dilvish gestured with his head. "That crevice runs most of the way up, and it is somewhat irregular on both sides."

"Looks to be a good choice. How will you get to it?"

"I'll begin climbing here. These handholds look good enough. I'll meet it at that first big break."

Dilvish unfastened his sword belt and slung it over his back. He chafed his hands again, then drew on his gloves.

"I might as well get started," he said. "Thanks, Black. I'll be seeing you."

"Good thing you're wearing those Elfboots," Black said. "If you slip you know that you'll land on your feet—eventually."

Dilvish snorted and reached for the first handhold.

Wearing a dark dress, wrapped in a green shawl,

the crone sat upon a small stool in the corner of the long underground chamber. Torches flamed and smoked in two wall sockets, melting—above and behind them—portions of the ice glaze that covered the walls and the ceiling. An oil lamp burned near her feet on the straw-strewn stone of the floor. She hummed to herself, fondling one of the loaves she bore in her shawl.

Across from her were three heavy wooden doors, bound with straps of rusted metal, small, barred windows set high within them. A few faint sounds of movement emerged from the one in the middle, but she was oblivious to this. The water that dripped from the irregular stone ceiling above the torches had formed small pools that spread into the straw and lost their boundaries. The dripping sounds kept syncopated accompaniment to her crooning.

". . . My little ones, my pretty ones," she sang. ". . . Come to Meg. Come to Mommy Meg."

There was a scurrying noise in the straw, in the dim corner near to the left-hand door. Hastily she broke off a piece of bread and tossed it in that direction. There followed a fresh rustling and a small movement. She nodded, rocked back on her seat, and smiled.

From across the way—possibly from behind the middle door—there came a low moan. She cocked her head for a moment, but it was followed by silence.

She cast another piece of bread into the same corner. The sounds that followed were more rapid, more pronounced. The straw rose and fell. She threw another piece, puckered her lips, and made a small chirping noise.

She threw more.

". . . . My little ones," she sang again, as over a dozen rats moved nearer, springing upon the bread, tearing at it, swallowing it. More emerged from dark places to join them, to contest for the food. Isolated squeaks occurred, increased in frequency, gradually merged into a chorus.

She chuckled. She threw more bread, nearer. Thirty or forty rats now fought over it.

From behind the middle door came a clinking of chain links, followed by another moan. Her attention, though, was on her little ones.

She leaned forward and moved the lamp to a position near the wall to her right. She broke another loaf and scattered its pieces on the floor before her feet. Small bodies rustled over the straw, approaching. The squeaking grew louder.

There came a heavy rattling of chains, a much louder moan. something moved within the cell and crashed against the door. It rattled, and another moan rose above the noises of the rats.

She turned her head in that direction, frowning slightly.

The next blow upon the door made a booming sound. For a moment, something like a massive eye seemed to peer out past the bars.

The moaning sound came again, almost seeming to shape itself into words.

". . . Meg! Meg . . ."

She half rose from her seat, staring at the cell door. The next crash—the loudest thus far—rattled it heavily. By then the rats were brushing against her legs, standing upon their hind paws, dancing. She reached out to stroke one, another . . . She fed them from her hands.

From within the cell the moaning rose again, this time working itself into strange patterns.

". . . Mmmmegg . . . Mmeg . . ." came the sound.

She raised her head once more and looked in that direction. She moved as if about to rise.

Just then, however, a rat jumped into her lap. Another ran up her back and perched upon her right shoulder.

"Pretty ones . . ." she said, rubbing her cheek against the one and stroking the other. "Pretty . . ."

There came a sound as of the snapping of a chain, followed by a terrific crash against the door across from her. She ignored it, however, for her pretty ones were dancing and playing for her. . . .

*   *   *

Reena drew garment after garment from her wardrobe. Her room was full of dresses and cloaks, muffles and hats, coats and boots, underthings and gloves. They lay across the bed and all of the chairs and two wall benches.

Shaking her head, she turned in a slow circle, surveying the lot. The second time around, she withdrew a dress from one of the heaps and draped it over her left arm. Then she took a heavy fur wrap down from a hook. She handed both to the tall, sallow, silent man who stood beside the door. His heavily wrinkled face resembled that of the man who had served her dinner—expressionless, vacant eyed.

He received the garments from her and began folding them. She passed him a second dress, a hat, hose, and underthings. Gloves . . . He accepted two heavy blankets she took down from a shelf. More hose . . . He placed everything within a duffellike sack.

"Bring it along—and one empty one," she said, and she moved toward the door.

She passed through and crossed the hallway to a stair, which she began to descend. The servant followed her, holding the sack by its neck with one hand, before him. He bore another one, folded, beneath his other arm, which hung stiffly at his side.

Reena made her way through corridors to a large, deserted kitchen, where a fire still smouldered beneath a grate. The wind made a whistling noise down the chimney.

She passed the large chopping block and turned left into the pantry. She checked shelves, bins, and cabinets, pausing only to munch a cookie as she looked.

"Give me the bag," she said. "No, not that one. The empty one."

She shook out the bag and began filling it—with dried meats, heads of cheese, wine bottles, loaves of bread. Pausing, she looked about again, then added a sack of tea and a sack of sugar. She also put in a small pot and some utensiles.

"Bring this one, too," she said finally, turning and departing the pantry.

She moved more cautiously now, the servant treading silently at her heels, a bag in either hand. She paused and listened at corners and stairwells before moving on. The only things she heard, though, were the screams from far above.

At length she came to a long, narrow stair leading down, vanishing into the darkness.

"Wait," she said softly, and she raised her hands, cupping them before her face, blowing gently upon them, staring at them.

A faint spark occurred between her palms, faded, grew again as she whispered soft words over it.

She drew her hands apart, her lips still moving. The tiny light hung in the air before her, growing in size, increasing in brilliance. It was blue white, and it reached the intensity of several candles.

She uttered a final word and it began to move, drifting before her down the stairwell. She followed it. The servant followed her.

They descended for a long while. The stair spiraled down with no terminus in sight. The light seemed to lead them. The walls grew damp, cold, colder, coming to be covered with a fine patina of frost figures. She drew her cloak farther forward over her shoulders. The minutes passed.

Finally they reached a landing. Distant walls were barely visible in the blackness beyond her light. She turned to her left and the light moved to precede her.

They passed through a long corridor that sloped gently downward, coming after a time to another stair at a place where the walls widened on either hand and the rocky ceiling maintained its level, to vanish from sight as they descended.

The full dimensions of the chamber into which they came were not discernible. It seemed more a cavern than a room. The floor was less regular than any over which they had so far passed, and it was by far the coldest spot they had yet come to.

Holding her cloak fully closed before her now, hands beneath it, Reena proceeded into the chamber, moving diagonally to her right.

Finally a large, boxlike sled came into view, a waxy rag hanging from the point of its left runner. It stood near the wall at the mouth of a tunnel through which an icy wind roared. The light came to hover above it.

Reena halted and turned to the servant.

"Put them in there," she said, gesturing, "toward the front."

She sighed as this was done, then leaned forward and covered them over with a pelt of white fur that had lain folded upon the vehicle's seat.

"All right," she said, turning away, "we'd better be getting back now."

She pointed in the direction from which they had come and the floating light moved to follow her finger.

In the circular room at the top of the highest tower, Ridley turned the pages in one of the great books. The wind howled like a banshee above the pitched roof, which sometimes vibrated with the force of its passage. The entire tower even had a barely perceptible sway to it.

Ridley muttered softly to himself as he fingered the leather binding, casting his eyes down the creamy sheets. He no longer wore the chain with the ring on it. These now rested atop a small chest of drawers by the wall near the door, a high, narrow mirror above it catching their image, the stone glowing palely within it.

Still muttering, he turned a page, then another, and paused. He closed his eyes for a moment, then turned away, leaving the book on the reading stand. He moved to the exact center of the room and stood there for a long while, at the middle of a red diagram drawn upon the floor. He continued to mutter.

He turned abruptly and walked to the chest of drawers. He picked up the ring and chain. He unfastened the chain and removed it.

Holding the ring between the thumb and forefinger of his right hand, he extended his left forefinger and quickly slipped the ring over it. He withdrew it almost immediately and took a deep breath. He regarded his reflection in the mirror. Quickly he slipped the ring on again, paused several moments, withdrew it more slowly.

He turned the ring and studied it. Its stone seemed to shine a little more brightly now. He fitted it over his finger once more, withdrew it, paused, refitted it, withdrew it, refitted it, paused, withdrew it, replaced it, paused longer, slowly slid it partway off, then back again. . . .

Had he been looking ahead into the mirror, he might have noticed that each manipulation of the ring caused a change in expression to flit across his face. He cycled between bafflement and pleasure, fear and satisfaction as the ring came on and off.

He slipped it off again and placed it atop the chest. He massaged his finger. He glanced at himself in the mirror, looked back down, staring deep into the depths of the stone. He licked his lips.

He turned away, walked several paces across the pattern, halted. He turned and looked back at the ring. He returned and picked it up, weighing it in the palm of his right hand.

He placed it upon his finger again and stood there wearing it, still gripping it tightly with the fingers of his other hand. This time his teeth were clenched and his brow furrowed.

As he stood there, the mirror clouded and a new image began to take shape within it. Rock and snow . . . Some sort of movement across it . . . A man . . . The man was crawling through the snow. . . . No.

The man's hands grasped at holds. He drew himself upward, not forward! He was climbing, not crawling!

The picture came clearer.

As the man drew himself up and located a fresh foothold, Ridley saw that he had on green boots. Then . . .

He snapped an order. There was a distancing effect. The man grew smaller, the cliff face wider and higher. There, above the climbing man, stood the castle, this castle, his own light gleaming through this tower window!

With a curse, he tore the ring from his finger. The

picture immediately faded, to be replaced by his own angry expression.

"No!" he cried, striding to the door and unfastening it. "No!"

He flung the door open and tore off down the winding stair.

Dilvish rested for a time, back and legs braced against the sides of the rock chimney, gloves in his lap, blowing on his hands, rubbing them. The chimney ended a small distance above his head. There would be no more resting after this until he reached the top, and then—who could tell?

A few flakes of snow drifted past him. He searched the dark sky, as he had been doing regularly, for a return of the flying creature, but saw nothing. The thought of it catching him in a vulnerable position had caused him considerable concern.

He continued to rub his hands until they tingled, until he felt some warmth returning. Then he donned his gloves again to preserve it. He leaned his head as far back as it would go and looked upward.

He had come over two thirds of the way up the vertical face. He sought and located his next handholds. He listened to his heartbeat, now returned to normal. Slowly, cautiously, he extended himself again, reaching.

He pushed himself upward. Leaving the chimney, he caught hold of a ledge and drew himself higher. His feet found purchase below him, and he reached again with one hand. He wondered whether Black had located a good way down. He thought of his last meal, cold and dry, almost freezing to his tongue. He recalled better fare from earlier days and felt his mouth begin to water.

He came to a slippery place, worked his way about it. He wondered at the strange feeling he had earlier, as if someone had been watching him. He had sought in the sky hurriedly, but the flying creature had been nowhere about.

Drawing himself over a thick, rocky projection, he

97

smiled, seeing that the wall began to slant inward above it. He found his footing and leaned into the climb.

He advanced more rapidly now, and before very long a sharp edge that could be the top came into view. He scrambled toward it as the slope increased, giving thought now to his movements immediately upon reaching it.

He drew himself up faster and faster, finally rising into a low crouch as the grade grew more gentle. Nearing what he took to be the top, he slowed again, finally casting himself flat a little more than a body length below the rim. For a time, he listened, but there were no sounds other than those of the wind.

Carefully, gloves in his teeth, he drew his sword belt over an arm and shoulder, up over his head. He unfastened it and lowered it. He adjusted his garments, then fitted it in place about his waist once again.

He moved very slowly, approaching the rim. When he finally raised his head above it his eyes were filled with the gleaming white of the castle, standing like a sugary confection not too far in the distance.

Several minutes passed as he studied the scene. Nothing moved but the snow. He looked for a side door, a low window, any indirect entrance. . . .

When he thought that he had found what he was seeking, he drew himself up over the edge and began his advance.

Meg sang to the dancing rats. The torches flickered. The walls ran wet. She teased the creatures with bits of bread. She stroked them and scratched them and chuckled over them.

There came another heavy crash against the central door. This time the wood splintered somewhat about the hinges.

"Mmeg . . . Mmeg . . . !" came from beyond it, and again the large eye appeared behind the bars.

She looked up, meeting the moist blue gaze. A troubled expression came over her face.

"Yes . . . ?" she said softly.

"Meg!"

There followed another crash. The door shuddered. Cracks appeared along its edge.

"Meg!"

Another crash. The door creaked and protruded beyond its frame, the cracks widened.

She shook her head.

"Yes?" she said more loudly, a touch of excitement coming into her voice.

The rats jumped down from her lap, her shoulders, her knees, racing back and forth across the straw.

The next crash tore the door free of its hinges, pushing it a full foot outward. A large, clawed, dead-white hand appeared about its edge, chain dangling from a metal cuff about its wrist, rattling against the wall, the door. . . .

"Meg?"

She rose to her feet, dropping the remainder of the bread from within her shawl. A black whirlwind of furry bodies moved about it, the squeaking smothering her reply. She moved forward through it.

The door was thrust farther outward. A gigantic, hairless white head with a drooping carrot of a nose looked out around it. Its neck was so thick that it seemed to reach out to the points of its wide shoulders. Its arms were as big around as a man's thighs, its skin a grease-splotched albino. It shouldered the door aside and emerged, back bent at an unnatural angle, head thrust forward, moving on legs like pillars. It wore the tatters of a shirt and the rent remains of a pair of breeches that, like their owner, had lost all color. Its blue eyes, blinking and watering against the torchlight, fixed upon Meg.

"Mack . . . ?" she said.

"Meg . . . ?"

"Mack!"

"Meg!"

She rushed to embrace the quarter ton of snowy muscle, her own eyes growing moist as he managed to hold her gently. They mumbled softly at one another.

Finally she took hold of his huge arm with her small hand.

"Come. Come, Mack," she said. "Food for you. Warm. Be free. Come."

She led him toward the chamber's exit, her pretty ones forgotten.

Ignored, the parchment-skinned servant moved about Reena's chambers on silent feet, gathering up strewn garments, restoring them to drawers and wardrobe. Reena sat at her dressing table, brushing her hair. When the servant had finished putting the room in order, he came and stood beside her. She glanced up, looked about.

"Very good," she said. "I have no further need of you. You may return to your coffin."

The dark-liveried figure turned and departed.

Reena rose and removed a basin from beneath the bed. Taking it to her nightstand, she added some water from a blue pitcher that stood there. Moving back to her dresser, she took up one of the candles from near the mirror and transferred it to a position to the left of the basin. Then she leaned forward and stared down at the moist surface.

Images darted there. . . . As she watched, they flowed together, fell apart, recombined. . . .

The man was nearing the top. She shuddered slightly as she watched him pause to unsling his blade and fasten it about his waist. She saw him rise further, to the very edge. She saw him survey the castle for a long while. Then he drew himself up, to move across the snow. . . . Where? Where would he seek entry?

. . . Toward the north and coming in closer, up toward the windows of that darkened storage room in back. Of course! The snow was banked highest there, and heavily crusted. He could reach the sill, draw himself up to climb upon it. It would only be the work of a few moments to knock a hole near the latch with the hilt of his weapon, reach through, and unfasten it. Then several long minutes with the blade to chip away all the ice that crusted the frame. More time to open it. Additional moments to locate the juncture of the shutters within, to slide the blade between them, lift upward, raise their latch . . . Then he would be disoriented in a dark room filled with clutter. It would take minutes more for him to negotiate that. . . .

She blew gently upon the surface of the water and the picture was gone among ripples. Taking up the candle, she bore it back to her dressing table, set it where it had been. She restored the basin to its former locale.

Seating herself before the mirror, she took up a tiny brush and a small metal box, to add a touch of color to her lips.

Ridley roused one of the servants and took him upstairs, to move along the corridor toward the room from which the screams still came. Halting before that door, he located the proper key upon a ring at his belt and unlocked it.

"At last!" came the voice from within. "Please! Now—"

"Shut up!" he said and turned away, taking the servant by the arm and turning him toward the open doorway immediately across the corridor.

He pushed the servant into the darkened room.

"Off to the side," he directed. "Stand there." He guided him further. "There—where you will be out of sight of anyone coming this way but can still keep an eye on him. Now take this key and listen carefully. Should anyone come along to investigate those screams, you must be ready. As soon as he begins to open that door, you are to emerge behind him quickly, strike him, and push him in through it—hard! Then close the door again quickly and lock it. After that you may return to your coffin."

Ridley left him, stepping out into the corridor where he hesitated a moment, then stalked off in the direction of the dining hall.

"The time is come," the face in the mirror announced, just as he entered.

He walked up to it, stared back at the grim visage. He took the ring into his hand and slipped it on.

"Silence!" he said. "You have served your purpose. Be gone now!"

The face vanished, just as its lips were beginning to form the familiar words anew, leaving Ridley to regard his own shadowy reflection surrounded by the ornate frame.

He smirked for an instant, then his face grew serious. His eyes narrowed, his image wavered. The mirror clouded and cleared again. He beheld the green-booted man standing upon a window ledge, chipping away at ice. . . .

He began to twist the ring. Slowly he turned it around and around, biting his lip the while. Then, with a jerk, he tore it from his finger and sighed deeply. The smirk returned to his reflected face.

He turned on his heel and crossed the room, where he passed through a sliding panel, a trapdoor, and down a ladder. Moving rapidly, down every shortcut he knew, he took his way once more to the servants' room.

Pushing the shutters aside, Dilvish stepped down into the room. A little light from the window at his back showed him something of the litter that resided there. He paused for several moments to memorize its disposition as best he could, then turned and drew the window shut, not closing it entirely. The heavily frosted panes blocked much of the light, but he did not want to risk betrayal by a telltale draft.

He moved silently along the map in his mind. He had sheathed his long blade and now held only a dagger in his hand. He stumbled once before he reached the door—against a jutting chair leg—but was moving so slowly that no noise ensued.

He inched the door open, looked to his right. A corridor, dark . . .

He stepped out into it and looked to the left. There was some light from that direction. He headed toward it. As he advanced, he saw that it came from the right—either a side corridor or an open room.

The air grew warmer as he approached—the most welcome sensation he had experienced in weeks. He halted, both to listen for telltale sounds and to relish the feeling. After several moments there came the tiniest clinking from around the corner. He edged nearer and waited again. It was not repeated.

Knife held low, he stepped forward, saw that it was the entrance to a room, saw a woman seated within it, reading a book, a glass of some beverage on the small table to her right. He looked to both the right and the left inside the doorway, saw that she was alone, stepped inside.

"You'd beter not scream," he said.

She lowered her book and stared at him.

"I won't," she replied. "Who are you?"

He hesitated, then: "Call me Dilvish," he said.

"My name is Reena. What do you want?"

He lowered the blade slightly.

"I have come here to kill. Stay out of my way and you won't be harmed. Get in it and you will. What is your place in this household?"

She paled. She studied his face.

"I am—a prisoner," she said.

"Why?"

"Our means of departure has been blocked, as has the normal means of entrance here."

"How?"

"It was an accident—of sorts. But I don't suppose you'd believe that."

"Why not? Accidents happen."

She looked at him strangely.

"That is what brought you, is it not?"

He shook his head slowly.

"I am afraid that I do not understand you."

"When he discovered that the mirror would no longer transport him to this place, he sent you to slay the person responsible, did he not?"

"I was not sent," Dilvish said. "I have come here of my own will and desire."

"Now it is I who do not understand you," said

103

Reena. "You say that you have come here to kill, and Ridley has been expecting someone to come to kill him. Naturally—"

"Who is Ridley?"

"My brother, the apprentice sorcerer who holds this place for his master."

"Your brother is apprentice to Jelerak?"

"Please! That name!"

"I am tired of whispering it! Jelerak! Jelerak! Jelerak! If you can hear me, Jelerak, come around for a closer look! I'm ready! Let's have this out!" he called.

They were both silent for several moments, as if expecting a reply or some manifestation. Nothing happened.

Finally Reena cleared her throat.

"Your quarrel, then, is entirely with the master? Not with his servant?"

"That is corect. Your brother's doings are nothing to me, so long as they do not cross my own purposes. Inadvertently, perhaps, they have—if he has barred my enemy's way to this place. But I can't see that as a cause for vengeance. What is this transport mirror you spoke of? Has he broken it?"

"No," she replied, "it is physically intact. Though he might as well have broken it. He has somehow placed its transport spell in abeyance. It is a gateway used by the master. He employed it to bring himself here—and from here he could also use it to travel to any of his other strongholds, and probably to some other places as well. Ridley turned it off when he was —not himself."

"Perhaps he can be persuaded to turn it back on again. Then when Jelerak comes through to learn the cause of the trouble, I will be waiting for him."

She shook her head.

"It is not that simple," she said. Then: "You must be uncomfortable, standing there in a knife-fighter's crouch. I know that it makes me uncomfortable, just looking at you. Won't you sit down? Would you care for a glass of wine?"

Dilvish glanced over his shoulder.

"Nothing personal," he said, "but I prefer to remain on my feet."

He sheathed his dagger, however, and moved toward the sideboard, where an open wine bottle and several glasses stood.

"Is this what you are drinking?"

She smiled and rose to her feet. She crossed the room to stand beside him, where she took up the botle and filled two glases from it.

"Serve me one, sir."

He took up a glass and passed it to her, with a courtly nod. Her eyes met his as she accepted it, raised it, and drank.

He held the other glass, sniffed it, tasted it.

"Very good."

"My brother's stock," she said. "He likes the best."

"Tell me about your brother."

She turned partly and leaned back against the sideboard.

"He was chosen as apprentice from among many candidates," she said, "because he possessed great natural aptitudes for the work. Are you aware that in its higher workings, sorcery requires the assumption of an artificialy constructed personality—carefully trained, disciplined, worn like a glove when doing the work?"

"Yes," Dilvish replied.

She gave him a sidelong look and continued:

"But Ridley was always different from most other people, in that he already possessed two personalities. Most of the time he is amiable, witty, interesting. Occasionally his other nature would come over him, though, and it was just the opposite—cruel, violent, cunning. After he began his work with the higher magics, this other side of himself somehow merged with his magical personality. When he would assume the necessary mental and emotional stances for his workings, it would somehow be present. He was well on his way to becoming a fine sorcerer, but whenever he worked at it he changed into something—quite unlikable. Still, this would be no great handicap, if he could put it off again as easily as he took it on—with the ring he had made for this purpose. But after a time, this—other—began to resist such a restoration. Ridley came to believe that *it* was attempting to control *him*."

"I have heard of people like that, with more than one nature and character," Dilvish said. "What finally happened? Which side of him came to dominate?"

"The struggle goes on. He is his better self now. But he fears to face the other—which has become a personal demon to him."

Dilvish nodded and finished his wine. She gestured toward the bottle. He refilled his glass.

"So the other was in control," Dilvish said, "when he nullified the spell on the mirror."

"Yes. The other likes to leave him with bits of unfinished work, so that he will have to call him back. . . ."

"But when he was—this other—did he say why he had done what he did to the mirror? This would seem more than part of a mental struggle. He must have realized that he would be inviting trouble of the most dangerous sort—from elsewhere."

"He knew what he was doing," she said. "The other is an extraordinary egotist. He feels that he is ready to meet the master himself in a struggle for power. The denatured mirror was meant to be a challenge. Actually he told me at the time that it was meant to resolve two situations at once."

"I believe that I can guess at the second one," Dilvish said.

"Yes," she replied. "The other feels that in winning such a contest, he will also emerge as the dominant personality."

"What do you think?"

She paced slowly across the room and turned back toward him.

"Perhaps so," she said, "but I do not believe that he would win."

Dilvish drained his glass and set it aside. He folded his arms across his breast.

"Is there a possibility," he asked, "that Ridley may gain control of the other before any such conflict comes to pass?"

"I don't know. He has been trying—but he fears the other so."

"And if he should succeed? Do you feel that this might increase his chances?"

"Who can say? Not I, certainly. I'm sick of this whole business and I hate this place! I wish that I were someplace warm, like Tooma or Ankyra!"

"What would you do there?"

"I would like to be the highest-paid courtesan in town, and when I grew tired of that perhaps marry some nobleman. I'd like a life of indolence and luxury and warmth, far from the battles of adepts!"

She stared at Dilvish.

"You've some Elvish blood, haven't you?"

"Yes."

". . . And you seem to know something of these matters. So you must have come with more than a sword to face the master."

Dilvish smiled.

"I bring him a gift from Hell."

"Are you a sorcerer?"

"My knowledge of these matters is highly specialized. Why?"

"I was thinking that if you were sufficiently skilled to repair the mirror, I could use it to depart and get out of everyone's way."

Dilvish shook his head.

"Magic mirrors are not my specialty. Would that they were. It is somewhat distressing to have come all this distance in search of an enemy and then to discover that his way here is barred."

Reena laughed.

"Surely you do not believe that something like that will stop him?"

Dilvish looked up, dropped his arms, looked about him.

"What do you mean?"

"The one you seek will be inconvenienced by this state of affairs, true. But it would hardly represent an insuperable barrier. He will simply leave his body behind."

Dilvish began to pace.

"Then what's keeping him?" he asked.

"It will first be necessary for him to build his power. If he is to come here in a disembodied state, he would be at a slight disadvantage in whatever conflict ensues. It becomes necessary that he accumulate power to compensate for this."

Dilvish turned on his heel and faced her, his back to the wall.

"This is not at all to my liking," he said. "Ultimately I want something that I can cut. Not some disembodied wraith! How long will this power-building go on, do you think? When might he arrive here?"

"I cannot hear the vibrations on that plane. I do not know."

"Is there some way that we could get your brother to—"

A panel behind Dilvish slid open and a mummy-faced servant with a club struck him across the back of the head. Staggered, Dilvish began to turn. The club rose and fell again. He sank to his knees, then slumped forward onto the floor.

Ridley pushed his way past the servant and entered the room. The club wielder and a second servant came in behind him.

"Very good, sister. Very good," Ridley observed, "to detain him here until he could be dealt with."

Ridley knelt and drew the long blade from the sheath at Dilvish's side. He threw it across the room. Turning Dilvish over, he drew the dagger from the smaller sheath and raised it.

"Might as well finish things," he said.

"You're a fool!" she stated, moving to his side and

taking hold of his wrist. "That man could have been an ally! He's not after you! It is the master he wants to slay! He has some personal grudge against him."

Ridley lowered the blade. She did not release his wrist.

"And you believed that?" he said. "You've been up here too long. The first man who comes along gets you to believe—"

She slapped him.

"You've no call to talk to me like that! He didn't even know who you were! He might have helped! Now he won't trust us!"

Ridley regarded Dilvish's face. Then he rose to his feet, his arm falling. He let go the dagger and kicked it across the floor. She released her grip on his wrist.

"You want his life?" he said. "All right. But if he can't trust us, we can't trust him either now." He turned to the servants, who stood motionless at his back. "Take him away," he told them, "and throw him down the hole to join Mack."

"You are compounding your mistakes," she said.

He met her gaze with a glare.

"And I am tired of your mocking," he said. "I have given you his life. Leave it at that, before I change my mind."

The servants bent and raised Dilvish's limp form between them. They bore him toward the door.

"Whether I was wrong or right about him," Ridley said, gesturing after them, "an attack will come. You know it. In one form or another. Probably soon. I have preparations to make, and I do not wish to be disturbed."

He turned as if to go.

Reena bit her lip, then said, "How close are you, to some sort of—accommodation?"

He halted, not looking back.

"Farther than I'd thought I might be," he replied, "at this point. I feel now that I do have a chance at dominating. This is why I can afford to take no risks here, and why I cannot brook any further interruptions or delays. I am returning to the tower now."

He moved toward the door, out of which Dilvish's form had just passed.

Reena lowered her head.

"Good luck," she said softly.

Ridley stalked out of the room.

The silent servants bore Dilvish along a dimly lit corridor. When they reached an indentation in the wall, they halted and lowered him to the floor. One of them entered the niche and raised a trapdoor. Returning to the still form, he helped to lift it then, and they lowered Dilvish, feet first, into the dark opening that had been revealed. They released him and he vanished from sight. One of them closed the trapdoor. They turned away and moved back along the corridor.

Dilvish was aware that he was sliding down an inclined surface. For a moment he had visions of Black's having slipped on the way up the mountain. Now he was sliding down the Tower of Ice, and when he hit the bottom . . .

He opened his eyes. He was seized by instant claustrophobia. He moved through darkness. He had felt the wall close beside him when he had taken a turn. If he reached out with his hands, he felt that the flesh would be rubbed away.

His gloves! He had tucked them behind his belt. . . .

He reached, drew them forth, began pulling them on. He leaned forward as he did so. There seemed to be a feeble patch of light ahead.

He reached out to his sides with both hands, spreading his legs as he did so.

His right heel touched the passing wall just as the palms of his hands did. Then his left . . .

Head throbbing, he increased the presure at all four points. The palms of his hands grew warm from the friction, but he slowed slightly. He pushed harder, he dug with his heels. He continued to slow.

He exerted his full strength now. The gloves were wearing through. The left one tore. His palm began to burn.

Ahead, the pale square grew larger. He realized that he was not going to be able to stop himself before he reached it. He pushed one more time. He smelled rotten straw, and then he was upon it.

He landed on his feet and immediately collapsed. The stinging in his left hand kept him from passing out. He breathed deeply of the fetid air. He was still dazed. The back of his head was one big ache. He could not recall what had happened.

He lay there panting as his heartbeat slowed. The floor was cold beneath him. Piece by piece, the memories began to return. . . .

He recalled his climb to the castle, his entry. . . . The woman Reena . . . They had been talking. . . .

Anger flared within his breast. She had tricked him. Delayed him until help arrived for dealing with him—

But her story had been so elaborately constructed, full of unnecessary detail. . . . He wondered. Was there more to this than a simple betrayal?

He sighed.

He was not ready to think yet. Where was he?

Soft sounds came to him across the straw. Some sort of cell perhaps . . . Was there another inmate?

Something ran across his back.

He jerked partway upright, felt himself collapsing, turned to his side as he did. He saw the small, dark forms in the dim light. Rats. That was what it had been. He looked about the half of the cell that he faced. Nothing else . . .

Rolling over onto his other side, he saw the broken door.

He sat up, more carefully than before. He rubbed his head and blinked at the light. A rat drew back at the movement.

He climbed to his feet, brushed himself off. He felt after his weapons, was not surprised to find them missing.

A wave of dizziness came and went. He advanced upon the broken door, touched it.

Leaning against the frame, he peered out into the

large room with frosty walls. Torches flickered in brackets at either end of it. There was an open doorway diagonally across from him, darkness beyond it.

He passed between the door and its frame, continuing to look about. There were no sounds other than the soft rat-noises behind him and the dripping of water.

He regarded the torches. The one to his left was slightly larger. He crossed to it and removed it from its bracket. Then he headed for the dark doorway.

A cold draft stirred the flames as he passed through. He was in another chamber, smaller than the one he had just quitted. Ahead he saw a stair. He advanced upon it and began to climb.

The stair took a single turn as he mounted it. At its top, he found a blank wall to his right, a wide, low-ceilinged corridor to his left. He followed the corridor.

After perhaps half a minute, he beheld what appeared to be a landing, a handrail jutting out of the wall above it. As he neared, he saw that there was an opening from which the railing emerged. Cautiously, he mounted the landing, listened for a time, peered around the corner.

Nothing. No one. Only a long, dark stair leading upward.

He transferred the torch, which was burning low, to his other hand and began to climb, quickly. This stair was much higher than the previous one, spiraling upward for a long while. He came to its ending suddenly, dropped the torch, and stepped upon its flame for a moment.

After listening at the top stair, he emerged into a hallway. This one had a long rug and wall decorations. Large tapers burned in standing holders along it. Off to his right, there was a wide stairway leading up. He moved to its foot, certain that he had come into a more frequented area of the castle.

He brushed his garments again, removed his gloves, and restored them to his belt. He ran his hand through his hair, while looking about for anything that might

112

serve as a weapon. Seeing nothing suitable, he commenced climbing.

As he reached a landing, he heard a blood-chilling shriek from above.

"Please! Oh, please! The pain!"

He froze, one hand on the railing, the other reaching for a blade that was not there.

A full minute passed. Another began. The cry was not repeated. There were no further sounds of any sort from that direction.

Alert, he began to move again, staying close to the wall, testing each step before placing his full weight upon it.

When he reached the head of the stair, he checked the corridor in both directions. It appeared to be empty. The cry had seemed to come from somewhere off to the right. He went that way.

As he advanced, a sudden soft sobbing began from some point to his left and ahead. He approached the slightly ajar door from behind which it seemed to be occurring. Stooping, he applied his eye to the large keyhole. There was illumination within, but nothing to view save for an undecorated section of wall and the edge of a small window.

Straightening, he turned to search again for some weapon.

The large servant's approach had been totally soundless, and he towered above him now, club already descending.

Dilvish blocked the blow with his left forearm. The other's rush carried him forward to collide with Dilvish, however, bearing him backward against the door, which flew wide, and through it into the room beyond.

Dilvish heard a cry from behind him as he strove to rise. At the same time the door was drawn shut, and he heard a key slipped into the lock.

"A victim! He sends me a victim when what I want is release!" There followed a sigh. "Very well . . ."

Dilvish turned as soon as he heard the voice, his memory instantly drawing him back to another place.

113

Bright red body, long, thin limbs, a claw upon each digit, it had pointed ears, backward-curving horns, and slitted yellow eyes. It crouched at the center of a pentacle, constantly shuffling its feet this way and that, reaching for him. . . .

"Stupid wight!" he snapped, lapsing into another tongue. "Would you destroy your deliverer?"

The demon drew back its arms, and the pupils of its eyes expanded.

"Brother! I did not know you in human form!" it answered in Mabrahoring, the language of demons. "Forgive me!"

Dilvish climbed slowly to his feet.

"I've a mind to let you rot there, for such a reception!" he replied, looking around the chamber.

The room was done up for such work, Dilvish now saw, everything still in its place. Upon the far wall there was a large mirror within an intricately worked metal frame. . . .

"Forgive!" the demon cried, bowing low. "See how I abase myself! Can you really free me? Will you?"

"First tell me how you came into this unhappy state," Dilvish said.

"Ah! It was the young sorcerer in this place. He is mad! Even now I see him in his tower, toying with his madness! He is two people in one! One day one must win over the other. But until then, he begins works and leaves them undone—such as summoning my poor self to this accursed place, forcing me upon this doubly accursed pentacle, and taking his thrice accursed self away without dismissing me! Oh! were I free to rend him! Please! The pain! Release me!"

"I, too, have known something of pain," said Dilvish, "and you will endure this for more questioning."

He gestured.

"Is that the mirror used for travel?"

"Yes! Yes, it is!"

"Could you repair the damage it has endured?"

"Not without the aid of the human operator who laid the counterspell. It is too strong."

114

"Very well. Rehearse your oaths of dismissal now and I will do the things necessary to release you."

"Oaths? Between us? Ah! I see! You fear I envy you that body you wear! Perhaps you are wise. . . . As you would. My oaths . . ."

". . . To include everyone in this household," Dilvish said.

"Ah!" it howled. "You would deprive me of my vengeance on the crazy sorcerer!"

"They are all mine now," Dilvish said. "Do not try to bargain with me!"

A crafty look came over the demon's face.

"Oh . . . ?" it said. "Oh! I see! Yours . . . Well, at least there will be vengeance—with much good rending and shrieking, I trust. That will be sufficient. Knowing that makes it much easier to renounce all claims. My oaths . . ."

It began the grisly litany, and Dilvish listened carefully for deviations from the necessary format. There were none.

Dilvish commenced speaking the words of dismissal. The demon hugged itself and bowed its head.

When he had finished, Dilvish looked back at the pentacle. The demon was gone from that place, but it was still present in the room. It stood in a corner, smiling an ingratiating smile.

Dilvish cocked his head.

"You are free," he said. "Go!"

"A moment, great lord!" it said, cowering. "It is good to be free and I thank you. I know, too, that only one of the greater ones of Below could have worked this release in the absence of a human sorcerer. So I would grovel and curry your favor a moment longer in the way of warning you. The flesh may have dulled your normal senses, and I bid you know that I feel the vibrations on another plane now. Something terrible is coming this way—and unless you are a part of its workings, or it of yours—I felt that you must be warned, great one!"

"I knew of it," Dilvish said, "but I am pleased that

you have told me. Blast the door's lock if you would do me a final service. Then you may go."

"Thank you! Remember Quennel in the days of your wrath—and that he served you here!"

The demon turned and seemed to blow apart like fog in a wind, to the accompaniment of a dull, roaring sound. A moment later there came a sharp, snapping noise from the direction of the door.

Dilvish crossed the room. The lock had been shattered.

He opened the door and looked out. The corridor was empty. He hesitated as he considered both directions. Then, with a slight shrugging movement, he turned to the right and headed that way.

He came, after a time, to a great, empty dining hall, a fire still smouldering upon its hearth, wind whistling down the chimney. He circled the entire room, moving along the walls, past the windows, the mirror, returnig to the spot from which he had begun, none of the wall niches proving doorways to anywhere else.

He turned and headed back up the corridor. As he did, he heard his name spoken in a whisper. He halted. The door to his left was partly ajar. He turned his head in that direction. It had been a woman' voice.

"It's me, Reena."

The door opened farther. He saw her standing there holding a long blade. She extended her arm.

"Your sword. Take it!" she said.

He took the weapon into his hands, inspected it, sheathed it.

". . . And your dagger."

He repeated the process.

"I am sorry," she said, "about what happened. I was as surprised as you. It was my brother's doing, not mine."

"I think I am willing to believe you," he said. "How did you locate me?"

"I waited until I was certain that Ridley was back in his tower. Then I sought you in the cells below, but you had already gone. How did you get out?"

"Walked out."

"You mean you found the door that way?"

"Yes."

He heard her sharp intake of breath, almost a gasp.

"That is not at all good," she said. "It means that Mack is certainly abroad."

"Who is Mack?"

"Ridley's predecessor as apprentice here. I am not certain what happened to him—whether he tried some experiment that simply did not work out, or whether his transformation was a punishment of the master's for some indiscretion. Whichever, he was changed into a dull-witted beast and had to be imprisoned down there, because of his great strength and occasional recollection of some noxious spell. His woman went barmy after that. She's still about. A minor adept herself, at one time. We've got to get out of here."

"You may be right," he said, "but finish the story."

"Oh. I've been looking all over for you since then. As I was about it, I noticed that the demon had stopped screaming. I came and investigated. I saw that he had been freed. I was fairly certain that Ridley was still in the tower. It *was* you, wasn't it?"

"Yes, I released it."

"I thought then that you might still be near, and I heard someone moving in the dining hall. So I hid in here and waited to see who it was. I brought you your weapons to show that I meant you no ill."

"I appreciate it. I am only now deciding what to do. I am sure you have some suggestions."

"Yes. I've a feeling that the master will come here soon and slay every living thing under these roofs. I do not want to be around when that occurs."

"As a matter of fact, he should be here very soon. The demon told me."

"It is hard to tell what you know and what you do not know," she said, "what you can do and what you cannot do. Obviously you know something of the arts. Do you intend to stay and face him?"

"That was my purpose in traveling all this distance,"

he replied. "But I meant to face him in the flesh, and if I did not find him here I meant to use whatever means of magical transportation might be present to seek him in others of his strongholds. I do not know how my special presents will affect him in a disembodied state. I know that my blade will not."

"You would be wise," she said, taking his arm, "very wise, to live to fight another day."

"Especially if you need my help in getting away from here?" he asked.

She nodded.

"I do not know what your quarrel with him may be," she said, leaning against him, "and you are a strange man, but I do not think you can hope to win against him here. He will have amassed great power, fearing the worst. He will come in cautiously—so cautiously! I know a possible way away, if you will help. But we must hurry. He could even be here right now. He—"

"How very astute of you, dear girl" came a dry, throaty voice from back up the hall, whence Dilvish had come.

Recognizing it, he turned. A dark-cowled figure stood just beyond the entrance within the dining hall.

"And you," he stated, "Dilvish! You are a most difficult person to be rid of, bloodling of Selar, though it has been a long while between encounters."

Dilvish drew his blade. An Awful Saying rose to his lips but he refrained from speaking it, not certain that what he saw represented an actual physical presence.

"What new torment might I devise for you?" the other asked. "A transformation? A degeneration? A—"

Dilvish began to move toward him, ignoring his words. From behind him he heard Reena whisper, "Come back. . . ."

He continued on toward the form of his enemy.

"I was nothing to you . . ." Dilvish began.

"You disturbed an important rite."

118

". . . and you took my life and threw it away. You visited a terrible vengeance upon me as casually as another man might brush away a mosquito."

"I was annoyed, as another man might be at a mosquito."

"You treated me as if I were a thing, not a person. That I cannot forgive."

A soft chuckle emerged from within the cowl.

"And it would seem that in my own defense now I must treat you that way again."

The figure raised its hand, pointing two fingers at him.

Dilvish broke into a run, raising his blade, recalling Black's spell of protection and still loathe to commence his own.

The extended fingers seemed to glow for a moment and Dilvish felt something like a passing wind. That was all.

"Are you but an illusion of this place?" the other asked, beginning to back away, a tiny quavering note apparent in his voice for the first time.

Dilvish swung his blade but encountered nothing. The figure was no longer before him. Now it stood among shadows at the far end of the dining hall.

"Is this thing yours, Ridley?" he heard him ask suddenly. "If so, you are to be commended for dredging up something I'd no desire whatever to recall. It shan't distract me, though, from the business at hand. Show yourself, if you dare!"

Dilvish heard a sliding sound from off to his left, and a panel opened there. He saw the slim figure of a younger man emerge, a shining ring upon the left forefinger.

"Very well. We shall dispense with these theatrics," came Ridley's voice. He seemed slightly out of breath and striving to control it. "I am master of myself and this place," he continued. He turned toward Dilvish. "You, wight! You have served me well. There is absolutely nothing more for you to do here, for it is between the two of us now. I give you leave to depart and assume your natural form. You may take the girl back with you as payment."

Dilvish hesitated.

"Go, I say! Now!"

Dilvish backed from the room.

"I see that you have cast aside all remorse," he heard Jelerak say, "and learned the necessary hardness. This should prove interesting."

Dilvish saw a low wall of fire spring up between the two of them. He heard laughter from the hall—whose, he was not certain. Then came a crackling sound and a wave of peculiar odors. Suddenly the room was a blaze of light. Just as suddenly it was plunged into darkness again. The laughter continued. He heard pieces of tile falling from the walls.

He turned away. Reena was still standing where he had left her.

"He did it," she said softly. "He has control of the other. He really did it. . . ."

"We can do no good here," Dilvish stated. "It is, as he said, between them now."

"But his new strength may still not be sufficient!"

"I'd imagine he knows that, and that that is why he wants me to take you away."

The floor shook beneath them. A picture dropped from a nearby wall.

"I don't know that I can leave him like that, Dilvish."

"He may be giving his life for you, Reena. He might have used his new powers to repair the mirror, or to escape this place by some other means. You heard how he put things. Would you throw away his gift?"

Her eyes filled with tears.

"He may never know," she said, "how much I really wanted him to succeed."

"I've a feeling he might," Dilvish said. "Now, how are we to save you?"

"Come this way," she said, taking his arm, as a hideous scream came from the hall, followed by a thunderclap that seemed to shake the entire castle.

Colored lights glowed behind them as she led him along the corridor.

"I've a sled," she said, "in a cavern deep below here. It is filled with supplies."

"How—" Dilvish began, and he halted, raising the blade that he bore.

An old woman stood before them at the head of the stair, glaring at him. But his eyes had slid beyond her, to behold the great pale bulk that slowly mounted the last few stairs, head turned in their direction.

"There, Mack!" she screamed suddenly. "The man who hit me! Hurt my side! Crush him!"

Dilvish directed the point of his blade at the advancing creature's throat.

"If he attacks me, I will kill him," he said. "I do not want to, but the choice is not mine. It is yours. He may be big and strong, but he is not fast. I have seen him move. I will make a very big hole, and a lot of blood will come out of it. I heard that you once loved him, lady. What are you going to do?"

Forgotten emotions flickered across Meg's features.

"Mack! Stop!" she cried. "He's not the one. I was wrong!"

Mack halted.

"Not—the—one?" he said.

"No. I was—mistaken."

She turned her gaze up the hallway to where fountains of fires flashed and vanished and where multitudes of cries, as of two opposing armies, rang out.

"What," she said, gesturing, "is it?"

"The young master and the old master," Reena said, "are fighting."

"Why are you still afraid to say his name?" Dilvish asked. "He's just up the corridor. It's Jelerak."

"Jelerak?" A new light came into Mack's eyes as he gestured toward the awful room. "Jelerak?"

"Yes," Dilvish replied, and the pale one turned away from him and began shuffling in that direction.

Dilvish looked about for Meg, but she was gone. Then he heard a cry of "Jelerak! Kill!" from overhead.

121

He looked up and saw the green-winged creature that had attacked him—how long ago?—flapping off in the same direction.

"They are probably going to their deaths," Reena said.

"How long do you think they have waited for such an opportunity?" he said. "I am sure that they know that they lost a long time ago. But just to have the chance now is winning, for them."

"Better in there than on your blade."

Dilvish turned away.

"I am not at all sure that *he* wouldn't have killed *me*," he said. "Where are we going?"

"This way."

She took him down the stair and up another corridor, heading toward the north end of the building. The entire place began shaking about them as they went. Furniture toppled, windows shattered, a beam fell. Then it was still again for a time. They hurried.

As they were nearing the kitchen, the place shook again with such violence that they were thrown to the floor. A fine dust was drifting everywhere now, and cracks had appeared in the walls. In the kitchen they saw that hot ashes had been thrown from the grate, to lay strewn about the floor, smoking.

"It sounds as if Ridley is still holding his own."

"Yes, it does," she said, smiling.

Pots and pans were rattling and banging together as they departed the kitchen, heading in the direction of the stairwell. The cutlery danced in its drawers.

They paused at the stair's entrance, just as a great, inhuman moan swept through the entire castle. An icy draft followed moments later. A rat flashed past them from the direction of the kitchen.

Reena signaled Dilvish to halt and, leaning against the wall, cupped her hands before her face. She seemed to whisper within them, and a moment after the small fire was born, to hover, growing, before her. She moved her hands outward and it drifted toward the stairwell.

"Come," she said to Dilvish, and she led the way downward.

He moved behind her, and from time to time the walls creaked ominously about them. When this happened, the light danced for a moment, and occasionally it faded briefly. As they descended, the sounds from above grew more muffled. Dilvish paused once, to place his hand upon the wall.

"Is it far?" he asked.

"Yes. Why?"

"I can still feel the vibrations strongly," he said. "We must be well below the level of the castle itself —down into the mountain by now."

"True," she replied, taking another turn.

"At first I feared that they might bring the castle down upon our heads. . . ."

"They probably *will* destroy the place if this goes on much longer," she said. "I'm very proud of Ridley —despite the inconvenience."

"That wasn't exactly what I meant," Dilvish said, as they continued their downward flight. "There! It's getting worse!" He put out a hand to steady himself as the stair shuddered from a passing shockwave. "Doesn't it seem to you that the entire mountain is shaking?"

"Yes, it does," she replied. "Then it must be true."

"What?"

"I'd heard it said that ages ago, at the height of his power, the ma—Jelerak—actually raised this mountain by his conjuring."

"So?"

"If he is sufficiently taxed in this place, I suppose that he might have to draw upon those ancient spells of his for more power. In which case—"

"The mountain might collapse as well as the castle?"

"There is that possibility. Oh, Ridley! Good show!"

"It won't be so good if we're under it!"

"True," she said, suddenly moving even faster. "As he's not *your* brother, I can see your point. Still, it must please you to see Jelerak so hard pressed."

123

"It does that," Dilvish admitted, "but you should really prepare yourself for any eventuality."

She was silent for a time.

Then: "Ridley's death?" she asked. "Yes. I've realized for some time now that there was a strong possibility of this, whatever the nature of their encounter. Still, to go out with such flare . . . That's something, too, you know."

"Yes," Dilvish replied. "I've thought of it many times myself."

Abruptly, they reached the landing. She turned immediately and led him toward a tunnel. The rocky floor trembled beneath them. The light danced again. From somewhere there came a slow, grinding sound, lasting for perhaps ten seconds. They rushed into the tunnel.

"And you?" she said, as they hurried along it. "If Jelerak survives, will you still seek him?"

"Yes," he said. "I know for certain that he has at least six other citadels. I know the approximate locations of several of them. I would seek them as I did this place."

"I have been in three of the others," she said. "If we survive this, I can tell you something about them. They would not be easy to storm either."

"It does not matter," Dilvish said. "I never thought that it would be easy. If he lives, I will go to them. If I cannot locate him, I will destroy them, one by one, until he must need come to me."

The grinding sound came again. Fragments of rocks fell about them. As this occurred, the floating light vanished before them.

"Remain still," she said. "I'll do another."

Several moments later another light glowed between her hands.

They continued on, the sounds within the rock ceasing for a time.

"What will you do if Jelerak is dead?" she asked him.

Dilvish was silent awhile. Then: "Visit my homeland," he said. "It has been a long while since I have been back. What will you do if we make it away from here?"

"Tooma, Ankyra, Blostra," she replied, "as I'd said, if I could find some willing gentleman to escort me to one of them."

"I believe that could be arranged," Dilvish said.

As they neared the end of the tunnel, an enormous shudder ran through the entire mountain. Reena stumbled; Dilvish caught her and was thrown back against the wall. With his shoulders, he felt the heavy vibrations within the stone. From behind them a steady crashing of falling rocks began.

"Hurry!" he said, propelling her forward.

The light darted drunkenly before them. They came into a cold cavern.

"This is the place," Reena said, pointing. "The sled is over there."

Dilvish saw the vehicle, took hold of her arm, and headed toward it.

"How high up the mountain are we?" he asked her.

"Two thirds of the way, perhaps," she said. "We are somewhat below the point where the rise steepens severely."

"That is still no gentle slope out there," he said, coming to a halt beside the vehicle and placing his hand upon its side. "How do you propose getting it down to ground level?"

"That will be the difficult part," she said, reaching within her bodice and withdrawing a folded piece of parchment. "I've removed this page from one of the books in the tower. When I had the servants build me this sled, I knew that I would need something strong to draw it. This is a fairly elaborate spell, but it will summon a demon beast to do our bidding."

"May I see it?"

She passed him the page. He unfolded it and held it near to the hovering light.

"This spell requires fairly lengthy preparations," he said a little later. "I don't believe we have that kind of time remaining, the way things are shaking and crumbling here."

"But it is the only chance we have," she said. "We'll need these supplies. I had no way of knowing that the whole damned mountain was going to start coming apart. We are simply going to have to risk the delay."

Dilvish shook his head and returned the page.

"Wait here," he said, "and don't start that spell yet!"

He turned and made his way along the tunnel down which icy blasts blew. Snow crystals lay upon the floor. After a single, brief turn, he saw the wide cave mouth, pale light beyond it. The floor there had a heavy coating of snow over ice.

He walked to the entrance and looked out, looked down. The sled could be edged over the lip of the ridge at his feet at a low place off to his left. But then it would simply take off, achieving a killing speed long before it reached the foot of the mountain.

He moved forward to the very edge, looked up. An overhang prevented his seeing anything above. He moved half a dozen paces to his left then, looked out, looked up, looked around. Then he crossed to the right-hand extremity of the ledge and looked up, shading his eyes against a blast of ice crystals.

There . . . ?

"Black!" he called, to a darker patch of shadow above and to the side. "Black!"

It seemed to stir. He cupped his hands and shouted again.

"Diiil . . . viish!" rolled down the slope toward him, after his own cry had died away.

"Down here!"

He waved both arms above his head.

"I . . . see . . . you!"

"Can you come to me?"

There was no answer, but the shadow moved. It came down from its ledge and began a slow, stiff-legged journey in his direction.

126

He remained in sight. He continued waving.

Soon Black's silhouette became clear through the swirling snow. He advanced steadily. He passed the halfway point, continued on.

As he came up beside him, Black pulsed heat for several moments and the snow melted upon him, trickling off down his sides.

"There are some amazing sorceries going on above," he stated, "well worth observing."

"Far better we do it from a distance," Dilvish said. "This whole mountain may be coming down."

"Yes, it will," Black said. "Something up there is drawing upon some very elemental, ancient spells woven all through here. It is most instructive. Get on my back and I'll take you down."

"It is not that simple."

"Oh?"

"There is a girl—and a sled—in the cave behind me."

Black placed his forefeet upon the ledge and heaved himself up to stand beside Dilvish.

"Then I had better have a look," he stated. "How did you fare up on top?"

Dilvish shrugged.

"All of that would most likely have happened without me," he said, "but at least I've the pleasure of seeing someone giving Jelerak a hard time."

"That's him up there?"

They started back into the cave.

"His body is elsewhere, but the part that bites has paid a visit."

"Who is he fighting?"

"The brother of the lady you are about to meet. This way."

They took the turn and headed back in the larger cave. Reena still stood beside the sled. She had wrapped herself in a fur. Black's metal hooves clicked upon the rock.

"You wanted a demon beast?" Dilvish said to her. "Black, this is Reena. Reena, meet Black."

Black bowed his head.

"I am pleased," he said. "Your brother has been providing me with considerable amusement while I waited without."

Reena smiled and reached out to touch his neck.

"Thank you," she said. "I am delighted to know you. Can you help us?"

Black turned and regarded the sled.

"Backward," he said after a time. Then: "If I were hitched facing it, I could draw back slightly and let it precede me down the mountain. You would both have to walk, though—beside me, holding on. I don't believe I could do it with you in the thing. Even this way it will be difficult, but I see it to be the only way."

"Then we'd better push it out and get started," Dilvish said, as the mountain shook again.

Reena and Dilvish each took hold of a side of the the vehicle. Black leaned against its rear. It began to move.

Once they reached the snow on the cave floor, it proceeded more easily. Finally they turned it about at the cave mouth and hitched Black between its traces.

Carefully, gently then, they edged its rear end over the ledge at the low place to the left as Black advanced slowly, maintaining tension on the traces.

Its runners struck the snow of the slope, and Black eased it down until it rested full length upon it. Gingerly he followed it then, jerking stiffly upright to anchor it after he had jumped the last few feet.

"All right," he said. "Come down now and take hold of me on either side."

They followed him and took up their positions. Slowly he began to advance.

"Tricky," he said as they moved. "One day they will invent names for the properties of objects, such as the tendency of a thing to move once it is placed in motion."

"Of what use would that be?" Reena asked. "Everybody already knows that that's what happens."

"Ah! But one might put numbers to the amount of

material involved and the amount of pushing required, and come up with wondrous and useful calculations."

"Sounds like a lot of trouble for a small return," she said. "Magic's a lot easier to figure."

"Perhaps you're right."

Steadily they descended, Black's hooves crunching through the icy crust. Later, when they finally reached a place from which they could view the castle, they saw that the highest tower and several low ones had fallen. Even as they watched, a section of wall collapsed. Fragments of it fell over the edge, fortunately descending the slope far to their right.

Beneath the snow the mountain itself was shaking steadily now, and had been for some time. Rocks and chunks of ice occasionally bounded past them.

They continued for what seemed an interminable time, Black edging the sled lower and lower with each step, Reena and Dilvish plodding numb-footed beside him.

As they neared the foot of the slope, a terrific crash echoed about them. Looking up, they saw the remains of the castle crumbling, shrinking, falling in upon itself.

Black increased his pace dangerously as small bits of debris began to rain about them.

"When we reach bottom," he said, "unhitch me immediately, but stay on the far side of the sled while you're doing it. I would be able to turn its side to the slope as we get there. Then, if you can hitch me properly in a hurry, do it. If the falling stuff becomes too severe, though, just crouch down on the far side and I will stand on the near one to help shield you. But if you can rehitch me, get in quickly and stay low."

They slid most of the final distance, and for a moment it seemed that the sled would turn over as Black maneuvered it. Picking himself up, Dilvish immediately set to work upon the harness.

Reena got behind the sled and looked upward.

"Dilvish! Look!" she cried.

Dilvish glanced upward as he finished the unfastening and Black backed out from between the traces.

The castle had completely vanished and large fissures had appeared in the slope. Above the summit of the mountain, two columns of smoke now stood—a dark one and a light one—motionless despite the winds that must be lashing at them.

Black turned and backed in between the traces. Dilvish began harnessing him again. More debris was now descending the slope, off to their right.

"What is it?" Dilvish said.

"The dark column is Jelerak," Black replied.

Dilvish looked back periodically as he worked, seeing that the two columns had begun to move, slowly, toward one another. Soon they were intertwined, though not merging, twisting and knotting about one another like a pair of struggling serpents.

Dilvish completed the harnessing.

"Get in!" he cried to Reena, as another part of the mountain fell away.

"You, too!" said Black, and Dilvish climbed in with her.

Soon they were moving, gathering speed. The top of the ice mass came apart as they watched, and still the billowing combatants rolled above it.

"Oh, no! Ridley seems to be weakening!" she said, as they raced away.

Dilvish watched as the dark column seemed to bear the lighter one downward into the heart of the falling mountain.

Black's pace increased, though chunks of rubble still skidded and raced about them. Soon both smoky combatants were gone from sight, high above them. Black moved faster yet, heading south.

Perhaps a quarter of an hour passed with no change in the prospect behind them, save for its dwindling. But crouched beneath the furs, Dilvish and Reena still watched. An air of anticipation seemed to grow over the entire landscape.

When it came, it rocked the ground, bouncing the sled from side to side, and its tremors continued for a long while after.

The top of the mountain blew off, peppering the sky with an expanding, dark cloud. Then the dusky smear was streaked, spread by the winds, sections of it reaching like slowly extending fingers to the west. After a time a mighty shock wave rolled over them.

Much later, a single, attenuated, rough-edged cloud —the dark one—separated itself from the haze. Trailing ragged plumes, jounced by the winds, it moved like an old man stumbling, fleeing southward. It passed far to the right of them and did not pause.

"That's Jelerak," Black said. "He's hurt."

They watched the rough column until it jerked out of sight far to the south. Then they turned again toward the ruin in the north. They watched until it faded from view, but the white column did not rise again.

Finally Reena lowered her head. Dilvish put his arm about her shoulders. The runners of the sled sang softly on their way across the snow.

DEVIL AND
THE DANCER

THE moon hung round and the cold winds blew when Oele danced for Devil, her footmarks traced in fire before the empty stone-faced altar. In the lands below it was already spring, but here in the mountains the night spoke of winter. Still, she danced barefooted, wearing but a flimsy gray garment belted with silver, more revealing than concealing her lithe figure as she raised the fires in ancient patterns, her long blond hair streaming about her.

The ground became a flickering tapestry, yet she was not burned. Far below on the northern slope, a ghostly palace quivered in the moonlight, towers fading to the point of transparency and regaining partial solidity moments later, walls moving to join with shadow and fleeing from it, lights waxing and waning behind high windows. The voice of the wind was a raw, shrieking thing, but neither did Oele feel the cold.

The darkness grew more dense above the altar until finally it blotted out stars. As this occurred, the wind died down and ceased. The flames sprang higher then, but the great blot above the stone was not illuminated thereby. It was a massive, rough-winged outline, great-headed and rippling. It seemed almost a hole in space itself, and she received the impression of enormous depths within it whenever her eyes passed that way.

She had danced thus, at certain seasons, down the years, beyond the memories of any who dwelled in the vicinity. All of these called her witch, and she, too, thought of herself in this fashion. The only one who knew more called her by a different title, though the distinction had become considerably frayed in the years since a dancing girl had slain her lover upon this spot to gain the powers he alone of all men had possessed. A priest he had been, the last surviving worshipper of an old god who, as a result, had valued him highly. Now Oele was the last worshipper, and she did not even know the god's name. She called him Devil and he granted her wishes in response to her choreographed acts of devotion, which she considered spells. A witch invoking a devil, a god responding to a worshipper, then—it was partly a matter of perspective, but only partly. For the things she asked of him were more in keeping with her own notions, and their relations were far removed from what his had been with his original worshippers long ago.

Yet between them the bond was strong. He drew strength from her dancing, from this final contact with the earth. And she also gained, many things.

At last her movements ceased and she stood amidst her design, facing the dark shape above the altar stone. For long moments a heavy stillness hung between them, until finally she spoke:

"Devil, I bring you my dance."

The figure seemed to nod, then to grow slightly. Finally, in a voice deep and slow, it replied:

"It is pleasing to me."

She waited, a ritualistically prolonged silence, then spoke again:

"My palace fades."

Again the pause, then the words "I know," followed by the gesture of a jagged, winglike member from the bottomless shadow, toward the place down the slope occupied by the wavering structure.

"Behold, priestess, it is firm once again."

She looked and saw that this was true. Now, in the moonlight, the palace stood still and substantial, its lights gleaming steadily, its ramparts thrusting prowlike against the night and the stars.

"I see," she finally replied. "But for how long will it remain thus? One by one my servants vanish, returning to the earth from which they sprang."

"They are with you once more."

"But for how long?" she repeated. "This is the third time I have had to call upon you to restore order—in less than a year."

The figure was silent much longer than the customary period.

"Tell me, Devil!"

"I cannot say for certain, priestess," it answered at last. "I have been growing weaker. Considerable energy is required to support yourself and your establishment for long periods—more than I can transform from your dance."

"What then is to be done?"

"You could choose a simpler way of life."

"I must have magnificence!"

"Soon I will lack the force to sustain it."

"Then you shall again have something stronger than my dancing!"

"I do not ask this."

"Yet you accept it when it becomes necessary."

"I accept it."

"Then you shall have sufficient man's blood to restore your powers, and to enhance my own."

There was silence.

"I begin now the closing dance," she stated, and as she commenced moving once again the flames died with each step that she retraced, the wind grew up about her, and the figure above the altar thinned and faded, giving back a fistful of stars.

When she had finished, she turned away and walked toward the palace without looking back. It was time to prepare for a journey, through the land below, to a seacoast town where it was said that anything one wanted could always be found.

The lady on the black-maned gray mare wore tan leather breeches and jacket and a brown and red cloak. Her hair and long-lashed eyes were dark and her wide mouth appeared to be faintly, perhaps unconsciously, working its way toward a smile. She wore a jade ring upon the middle finger of her left hand, an onyx one upon her right. A short sword hung from her belt.

Her companion wore black breeches and green jacket and boots. His cloak was black, lined with green, and he wore a sword and dagger at his waist. He sat astride a black, horse-shaped creature whose body appeared to be of metal.

The two of them led three pack horses up the mountain trails through the brisk, clear afternoon air. The sound of running water came to their ears from somewhere ahead.

"The weather improves daily," the lady remarked.

"After the regions we've traveled through, this seems almost summerish."

"Once we've quitted these heights," the man replied, "things should be even more comfortable. And when we reach the coast it could almost be balmy. We'll get you to Tooma at a good time of year."

The lady looked away.

"I am no longer so eager to reach the place . . ."

Bearing to the right, they rounded a rocky promontory. The man's mount made a strange noise. Turning his head, the rider scanned the trail.

"We are not alone," he observed.

She followed his gaze to where a man was seated upon a rock ahead and to the right. His hair and beard were pure white and he was dressed in animal skins. As they watched him, he stood, leaning upon a staff that was taller than himself.

"Hello," he hailed.

"Greetings," said the green-booted rider, coming to a halt before him. "How fare you?"

"Well enough," the man replied. "Do you travel far?"

"Yes. Down to Tooma, at least."

The man nodded.

"You'll not be out of these hills tonight."

"I know. I glimpsed a castle far ahead. Perhaps they'll let us sleep within its walls."

"Mayhap they will. For its mistress, Oele, has always been kindly disposed toward travelers, with a liking for whatever tales they bring. I am, as a fact, headed that way myself, to partake of the place's hospitality—though I've heard the lady is traveling at the moment. That beast you ride has a most unusual appearance, sir."

"He has indeed."

". . . And you've a somewhat familiar look, if I may say it. May I ask your name?"

"I am Dilvish, and this is Reena."

The lady nodded and smiled.

"Not a common name, yours. There was a Dilvish, long ago. . . ."

"I do not believe that castle stood in those days."

"To be sure, it did not. This was then the home of a hill tribe, reasonably content with its flocks and its god—whose name has since been forgotten. But the cities grew up below and—"

"Taksh'mael," Dilvish said.

"What?"

"Taksh'mael was their god," Dilvish answered, "keeper of the flocks. A friend and I once laid an offering on his altar when we passed this way—long ago. I wonder whether the altar still stands."

"Oh, it does, where it has always stood. . . . You are definitely a member of a minority to have it in mind at all. Perhaps 'twere better you did not stop at the castle. . . . Seeing the area come upon such bad times could not but depress one such as yourself. On second thinking, I'd say ride on and clear this poor place from your mind. Remember it as once it was."

"Thank you, but we have traveled a great distance," Dilvish replied. "It does not seem worth the extra effort merely to preserve a few sensibilities. We will go to the castle."

The man's large, pale eyes fixed him, then jerked away. With one hand he groped beneath his shaggy garments, then he limped forward, extending that hand toward Dilvish.

"Take this," he muttered. "You should have it."

"What is it?" Dilvish asked, automatically reaching down.

"A trifle," said the other. "An old thing I've had a long while, a mark of the god's favor and protection. One who remembers Taksh'mael ought to have such hereabouts."

Dilvish examined it, a fragment of gray stone veined with pink, into which the image of a ram had been scratched. It was pierced on one end and a worn woolen strand passed through this aperture.

"Thank you," he said, reaching for his bag. "I'd like to give you something in return."

"No," said the old man, turning away. " 'Tis a

freely given gift, and I've no use for citified geegaws. And 'tis not much for all that. The newer gods can afford much fancier, I'm certain."

"Well, may he guard your footsteps."

"At my age, I doubt it matters. Fare thee well."

He hiked off among the rocks and was soon gone from sight.

"Black, what do you make of it?" Dilvish asked, leaning forward to dangle the charm before his mount.

"There is some power in it," Black replied, "but it is of a tainted magic. I am not at all sure that I would trust anyone who bestows such a thing."

"First he told us to stop at the castle, then he told us to pass it by. On which piece of advice shall we mistrust him?"

"Let me see it, Dilvish," Reena said.

He dropped it into her hands and she studied it for a long while.

"True, it is as Black says . . ." she finally began.

"Should I keep it or throw it away?"

"Oh, keep it," she replied, passing it back. "Magic is like money. Who cares where it comes from? It's what you spend it on that counts."

"That is only true if you can control the expenditure," he said. "Do you want to stop at the castle? Or shall we travel as far as we can tonight?"

"The animals are getting tired."

"True."

"I believe he was a bit dotty."

"Most likely."

"A real bed would be very nice."

"Then we shall visit the castle."

Black was silent as they moved ahead.

Oil lamps, candles, and a large fireplace lit the tavern where Oele danced. Sailors, tradesmen, soldiers, and assorted rogues and citizens drank and dined at the heavy wooden tables. Tonight she wore her blue and green costume, and two musicians accompanied her energetic movements in the cleared area at the

137

rear of the main room. Business had improved considerably since she had come to town two weeks earlier, and though she had received three proposals of marriage and many other sorts of offers, yet did she remain unattached. Nor did her lack of a hardy male companion result in many difficulties. A steady gaze and a single, imperious gesture terminated the undesired attentions of the most importunate, causing a man to drop senseless to the ground. It was obvious that she did not desire the beery embraces of most patrons of the place, though her eyes searched every face during the course of an evening. And now there were some new ones. A caravan had come in from the west that afternoon, and a ship had arrived from southern waters. Tonight's crowd was even noisier than usual.

One tall son of the desert drew her eyes—slow-moving, dark, and hawkish. His flowing garments did not conceal his sturdy, well-proportioned frame. He took his ease near the doorway, sipping wine and smoking from a complicated contraption he had set upon the table before him. A number of similarly garbed men were seated at the same table, conversing in their sibilant tongue. The tall man's eyes never left her, and she began to feel that he might be the one. There were signs of great vitality in even the smallest of his movements.

A group of sailors arrived as the evening wore on, but she ignored them. By then she was dancing only for the one she had chosen. And it became apparent from the light in his eyes, his smile, and the words he had spoken as she passed near that he was captivated. He would be a fine one. Another hour and she would take him away. . . .

"Move it this way, lady. I like it."

She glanced to her right toward the man who had spoken and saw blue eyes beneath a wild thatch of coppery hair, a gold earring, very white teeth, a red neckerchief—one of the sailors who had just come in.

It was difficult to judge his size, leaned forward the way he was.

She did move nearer, studying him. Interesting scar on his chin . . . Big, capable hands on the table before him . . .

She moved her lips through a faint smile. He was more animated than the other, and certainly as filled with life. She wondered . . .

She heard a noise at her back and turned without missing a step. The trader was standing, glaring at the sailor. His men were also rising. She continued to smile and turned away again. The music died abruptly. She heard an oath, loud in the sudden stillness.

"You're a live one," the sailor said, getting to his feet. "I hope you're worth it."

All at once the entire room seemed to be in motion as tables and seats were upset. The sailors and traders moved toward one another, blades appearing almost magically in their hands. The other patrons scurried to sheltered vantages or quit the establishment entirely via the nearest exits. Showing no fear, Oele removed herself several paces, to make room for the combat.

The sailor she watched was moving forward in a low crouch, a stiletto in his right hand. The tall trader brandished a longer, curved blade. As their men struggled with one another about them, they pushed their way toward a cleared area nearer the center of the room as if by mutual consent. From somewhere a flagon sped toward the back of the trader's head. Oele gestured sharply and it veered off to shatter against the wall.

The sailor rolled away from the first slash of the other's blade and riposted instantly with a high overhand thrust that nicked the man's biceps. He could not dodge the countercut, however, but managed to parry it with his own weapon. He danced away then, unable to counterthrust beyond the other's greater length of blade. He began to circle him widdershins, his feet shuffling and stamping. As his back was for a moment exposed to the general melee, a small trader rushed toward him. Oele gestured again and it was as if the shorter man had been seized by a giant hand and cast sideways across the room. She smiled and licked her lips.

In circling, the sailor's foot encountered a small stool. He kicked it toward the other. Despite his lengthy garments, however, the trader avoided it with a quick movement and cut again toward his opponent's head. But the sailor had drawn a belaying pin from his sash, and he blocked the blow with it, moved in rapidly, and thrust toward the other's belly.

The trader managed to recover and parry in time, but it left him in an awkward position at very close quarters. The belaying pin struck him on the side of the head. He fell back, obviously dazed, swinging a wide parry, and the club took him again, high upon the left cheekbone. He stumbled and the club rose and fell twice more in rapid succession. He sprawled upon the floor and lay unmoving, garments disarrayed. The sailor advanced and kicked the blade from his extended hand. Still he did not stir. Breathing heavily, the seaman wiped his brow and smiled up at Oele, thrusting the pin back into his sash.

"Well done," she said. "Almost."

He glanced at his blade, then shook his head.

"It's done," he said. "I'll not be sticking him just for your amusement."

He placed his blade back into a sheath on the side of his right boot. The fighting between the sailors and the traders still continued behind him but already showed some signs of slowing, losing force. After one quick glance in that direction, the seaman bowed to Oele.

"Captain Reynar," he said, "at your service. Master of my own vessel, *Tiger's Foot*." He extended his arm. "Come now and I'll show her to you. I think you might enjoy cruising the southern waterways."

She took his arm and they turned.

"I think not," she said. "For I, too, rule in my own

place, which I am not about to forsake. Shall we save these poor fellows from further injury?"

She made a sweeping gesture toward the remaining combatants, and they all fell unconscious to the floor.

"Now that's a fine trick," he said, "and one which I wouldn't mind knowing."

She gestured again as they advanced and the door swung open before them.

"Perhaps I'll teach you," she answered, as they passed outside. "But my rooms are nearer than your ship and doubtess less cramped—though we'll be leaving them in the morning on a journey to the heights."

He grinned at her.

"It would take a lot to persuade a captain to desert his vessel—with no disrepect to your obvious charms."

"Cup your hands."

He released her arm and did so. She covered his hands with her own and a clinking sound began. Moments later he strained at an unexpected weight. She raised her hands and his were filled with gleaming coins. More continued to drop into them, spilling over and falling to the ground.

"Stop! Stop! They're getting away!" he cried.

She laughed, a sound not unlike the rattle of the gold, but the deluge of money ceased. He began stowing the coins in various places about his person. He knelt and recovered the fallen ones. He examined them. He bit one.

"Real! They're real!" he said.

"What were you saying about a captain and his ship?"

"You've no idea how wretched a thing the seafaring life can be. I've always wanted to live in the mountains." He touched his brow and offered his arm again. "Which direction?" he asked.

The sun had passed behind the mountain, casting long shadows, though day still lay upon the land below when Dilvish and Reena approached the castle they had seen hours earlier.

141

They halted and stared at it. Pennants were flapping upon battlements and tower tops and there seemed to be a light behind every window. The portcullis was raised and a faint sound of music came from within.

"What do you think?" Dilvish said.

"I was comparing it to the castle that was my home," Reena replied. "It looks fine to me."

They peered in through the gate. A woman who had been waiting near it stepped through and hailed them:

"Travelers! You are welcome here if you are seeking shelter."

Dilvish gestured toward the trappings upon the walls, toward the long carpet that he now saw stretched beyond the gate.

"What is the occasion," he asked, "for the display?"

"Our mistress has been away," the woman replied. "She will return tonight with her new consort."

"She must be a remarkable woman, to keep such an establishment in this place."

"She is indeed, sir."

Dilvish stared a moment longer.

"I've a mind to stay here," he finally said.

". . . And I've a body that would welcome some ease," Reena told him.

"Let's go."

They advanced until they reached the squat, dark-haired woman who had called to them. Her hands were large, her movements deliberate; her face was peppered with moles. She smiled a large-toothed smile and conducted them within.

Dilvish counted five other servants—two women and three men—laboring at various chores in the courtyard. Among these, several were hanging additional decorations. The woman who had welcomed them called to one of the men.

"He will take care of your horses," she stated. Then she turned and eyed Black. "Except for this one. What do you wish done with him?"

Dilvish glanced toward a small corner area off to his left.

"If I might, I would leave him over there," he said. "He will not move."

"You are certain?"

"I am certain."

"Very well. Do it. Set aside the things you would have taken in and I will help you bear them to your chamber. You will dine at the mistress's table later."

"In that case, I'll want that larger one," Reena said, indicating a pack, while Dilvish and Black moved off toward the chosen corner.

"I am vaguely troubled," Black said, "by our meeting with that old man. So I will not wander off from this body while it stands here. Should you need me, summon me and I will come."

"All right," Dilvish said, "though I doubt I will need to."

Black snorted and grew still, becoming a statue of a horse. Dilvish dismounted, hefted his gear, and followed the others inside.

The woman who had met them, whose name they had learned was Andra, conducted them to a third-floor chamber overlooking the courtyard.

"When the mistress and her man arrive, we will summon you to dinner and an entertainment," she said. "In the meantime, is there anything you might need?"

Dilvish shook his head.

"Thank you, no. I am curious, though, how you know exactly when she will arrive. You seem fairly far removed from most other places."

Andra looked puzzled.

"She is the mistress," she replied. "We know."

After she had departed, Dilvish nodded toward the door.

"Strange . . ." he said.

"Perhaps not," Reena replied. "There *is* a peculiar feeling to this place. I should recognize it if anyone should, though it is not as strong as it was in my former home. I believe this Mistress Oele might be a minor adept of some sort. Even her servants all seem to have the dull responsiveness of someone under control."

"You have never heard of her, though—or of anyone in this vicinity—as a sister in the Art?"

"No. But there are so many lesser practitioners about that one cannot keep track of them all. Only the doings of the big ones provide general subjects for gossip."

"Such as those of your former employer?"

She turned toward him, eyes narrowed.

"Must you turn every conversation back to your enemy and your revenge?" she said. "I hate him, too, and I know he put you through a lot. He also killed my brother! But I'm sick of hearing about him!"

"I—I am sorry," he replied. "I suppose that I have become somewhat single-minded. . . ."

She laughed.

" 'Somewhat'?" she said. "Do you live for anything else? Do you ever listen to yourself? The way he controls your every thought, your every action, you might as well be under his spell! If you succeed in destroying him, what then? Is there anything else left of your life? You—"

She broke off and turned away.

"I am sorry," she said. "I shouldn't have said any of that."

"No," he replied, not looking at her. "You're right. I never noticed. But you are right. Would you believe that I was raised to be a courtier—that I played music and sang, wrote poetry . . . ? I did other things later because of circumstances, but my birth was gentle. It was only by accident that I developed certain military aptitudes, and necessity that furthered such a career. I had always intended—something else. Now . . . How long ago all that seems! You have said something true. I wonder . . ."

"What?"

"What I *would* do if it were all over. Return to my homeland perhaps, try to resolve some ancient wrongs against our house—"

"Another vendetta?"

He laughed, a thing she had seldom heard.

"More likely a matter of dull legalities. I *am* going to think about it, and a lot of other things, now. Even the big—gap—in my life has shifted a bit, from nightmare to dream. Yes, I should occasionally concern myself with other matters."

"Such as?"

"What to do until dinner time, for one."

"I'll help you think of something," she told him, coming across the room.

The torches blazed and crackled and the sounds of music were all about them as Reynar and Oele entered her courtyard, riding across the long carpet, garlanded with flowers her servants had cast upon them as they passed through the gate. Oele nodded and smiled and the shadows danced and slithered. Then her expression froze as her gaze fell upon a dark shape in a distant corner, metallic highlights upon its surface. She drew rein and pointed.

"What," she asked in a loud voice, "is that?"

Andra rushed to her side.

"It belongs to a guest, mistress," she stated, "a man named Dilvish, who came by earlier. I offered hospitality, as you have always wished."

Oele dismounted, handing Andra the reins. She crossed the courtyard and stood before Black. Then she circled him, still staring. Finally she put out a jeweled hand and slapped his shoulder. A ringing sound followed. She backed away, then returned to Andra.

"How," she said, "did he transport a statue of a horse through the mountains? And why?"

"Well, it is a statue now, ma'am," Andra replied, "but he rode in on it. Said it wouldn't move when he left it there. It hasn't."

Oele looked back at Black. In the meantime, Reynar had dismounted and moved to her side.

"What is the matter?" he asked.

She took his hand and led him across the yard toward the main doorway.

"That—thing," she said, with a jerk of her head, "bore its master here earlier."

"How can that be?" Reynar asked. "It looks pretty stiff to me."

"Obviously our guest is a sorcerer," she replied. "I find this more than a little awkward."

"How so?"

"We hurried to get home today because it is tonight when the moon stands full in high heaven that I must do the things to insure the power of which I spoke."

"To grant me powers like your own?"

She smiled.

"Of course."

They mounted a stair and passed into a large entrance hall. There was more music, from somewhere off to the left. Reynar sniffed exotic perfumes.

"And this sorcerer . . . ?" he inquired.

"I don't care for the idea of having one of his sort about just now. His arrival is strangely timed."

Reynar smiled as she led him toward a stair.

"It may be that I can arrange the time of his departure to suit your taste," he said.

She patted his arm.

"Let us not be too hasty. We will dine with the man and take his measure shortly."

She led him up the stairway and into her chambers, where she rang for a servant. A woman resembling Andra, though taller and heavier, answered the summons.

"When," Oele asked her, "will dinner be ready?"

"As soon as you wish, ma'am. They are all dishes of a sooner or later sort. The meat has been turning slowly on a low flame for some time."

"We shall dine an hour hence. Ask the man to join us."

"Only the man, ma'am? Not his woman?"

"I did not realize that there were two of them. Say me their names."

"He is called Dilvish, and his lady is Reena."

"I've heard that name before," Reynar said. "Dilvish . . . It seemed familiar when the other one mentioned it out in the yard. A military man, perhaps?"

"I do not know," the woman answered.

"Of course you are to tell Reena also," Oele said. "Go and do it now."

The woman departed and Oele laid out her clothing for the evening—a surprisingly simple gray garment and a silver belt. She stepped behind a screen where water and towels awaited her, and shortly after that Reynar heard splashing sounds.

"What do you know of this man?" she finally called out.

Reynar, who had crossed to the window and was staring out over the yard, turned.

"I believe he is said to have distinguished himself at a place called Portaroy," he answered, "in those interminable East–West border wars. Something about his riding a metal horse and having raised an army of the dead. But I don't recall the details. I know nothing of the woman."

"He's a long way from Portaroy," she said. "I wonder what he is doing here?"

He moved to her dressing table where he combed his hair and cleaned his fingernails. He located a nondescript piece of cloth and began wiping his boots with it.

"Uh—if he is here for something which might be at cross-purposes with your own plans for tonight," he said, "can you deal with—something like that?"

"Do not worry yourself," she replied. "I am not without certain resources. I'll take care of you."

"I never doubted it," he said, smiling and polishing his belt buckle.

Reena had changed into a long, décolleté green dress with black trim and puffed sleeves, Dilvish into a brown blouse and soft green leather vest, his black trousers belted with matching green. They heard the music from the dining hall as they descended the stair —strings and a flute, slow. Soon the cooking odors reached them.

"I'm anxious to meet our hostess," Dilvish stated.

"I must confess I am more anxious to make the acquaintance of a warm meal," Reena said. "How long since that last inn? Over a week . . ."

Smiling, Oele rose when her guests entered. Reynar hastened to imitate her. The introductions were brief, and she bade Dilvish and Reena be seated. Servants moved to bring in the first course and to pour wine. A fire crackled on the hearth, across from Dilvish, behind Reena. The musicians were stationed at the far end of the room.

They had been eating for several minutes before Dilvish realized that there was another diner, not in their company. At a small table at the far side of the fireplace sat an old man clad in skins, his staff leaning against the wall. It appeared to be the same man who had met them on the trail earlier. When their eyes met, he smiled and nodded. The man gestured toward his throat and Dilvish touched the charm inside his shirt and nodded back.

"I hadn't noticed the old man," Dilvish remarked.

"Oh, he's been by before," Oele said. "Keeps flocks. Passes this way occasionally. Reynar tells me that he believes he recalls your name in connection with a place called Portaroy. Did he get it right?"

Dilvish nodded.

"I fought there."

"I've begun remembering stories I've heard," Reynar said. "Is it true that the metal beast you ride is really a demon who helped you to escape from Hell and that one day he will carry you off?"

"He carries me off almost every day," said Dilvish, smiling, "and he has helped me in many ways—and I, him."

". . . And there was some business about a statue. Is it true that you once were one—as the beast is now?"

Dilvish looked down at his hands.

148

"Yes," he said softly.

"Extraordinary," Oele remarked. "Might I ask what brings a man of your—background—so far from the scene of your triumphs?"

"Revenge," he said, beginning to eat again. "I am on my way to find someone who has caused me and a great number of other people a good deal of trouble."

"Who might that be?" Reynar asked.

"I do not wish to bring a curse upon this place by mentioning his name in it. He is a sorcerer."

"You seem to find yourself bad enemies," Reynar said. "We've that in common. I slew a sorcerer once, in the Eastern Isles. Damn near suffocated me before I could reach him. He'd stopped my breathing. Fortunately, I'd had some experience at pearl diving. . . ."

Dilvish turned his attention back to his meal. A fresh question every now and then kept the sailor talking about his voyages. From the corner of his eye, Dilvish noted signs of growing exasperation on Oele's part, but she seemed to restrain herself each time he had thought her ready to silence the man. Then Dilvish realized from the direction of his smiles that Reena seemed to be listening to him with a growing fascination, even to the neglect of her food; nor were his smiles unreturned. Dilvish glanced at Oele and she quirked an eyebrow at him. He shrugged.

Suddenly everything about her was extremely beautiful and desirable. Far more so than moments before. He recognized the feeling, though the knowledge in no way detracted from the impression. Glamourie. He had felt it years before in his homeland. She was magically enhancing her natural appeal. Yet it lasted for but a moment, faded, and left her as she had been. What had been its purpose; he wondered. A promise? An invitation?

When they had finished eating, Oele rose, fixed him with her eyes, and said, "Come dance with me."

He got to his feet and moved alongside the table toward the vacant area at the end of the room near

149

the musicians. As he did, he saw that Reena and Reynar were also rising.

He took Oele's hand and began to move to the music—stately, slow. It was a variation of something he had learned long ago, and he quickly met the rhythms. Oele moved with considerable grace, and whenever she faced him she was smiling. She seemed to be moving nearer on each such occasion.

"Your wife is very lovely," she said.

"She is not my wife," he replied. "I am escorting her to a city in the south."

". . . And after that?"

"I will be about the business I mentioned earlier. I've no desire to expose another to the danger."

"Interesting," she said, turning away again. When next she faced him, she continued, "I gather you do not care to speak much about such things, but are you a binder of demons? Can you control them?"

Dilvish studied her face, learned nothing from it.

"Yes," he finally said. "I've some experience in the area."

After several more beats of the music, he asked, "Why?"

"If you were to succeed in binding a truly strong one to your will," she said, "might it not serve you well in this struggle with your sorcerer?"

"Possibly," he replied, raising her hand and lowering it again.

She brushed against him.

"It would be better," she said, "to control such a one than to have it control you, to order it about without having to pay it first—wouldn't you say?"

He nodded.

"That applies to most servants and services, doesn't it?" he said.

"Of course," she agreed. Then: "I have such a one about. . . ."

"Here? In the castle?" Dilvish almost halted.

She shook her head.

"Nearby."

150

"And you want me to subdue it?"

"Yes."

"Do you know its name?"

"No. Is that important?"

"It is essential. I had assumed you knew something of these matters."

"Why?"

"There is that about you which bespeaks some involvement with such forces."

"I pay for my powers, but I do not understand them. I am tired of paying. If I get you the name will you take control of the devil and remain here with me?"

". . . And Reena?"

"You said that she is not important, that you will be disposing of her shortly. . . ."

"I did not say that she is not important. What of Reynar . . . ?"

"He is not important."

Dilvish was silent for several measures. Then: "If you merely wish to be rid of your demon, I might be able to manage it without the name," he said.

"I do not wish to be rid of it. I want to establish complete control over it."

"I am not at all sure your demon would be that beneficial to me, but if you had the name I might be persuaded to stay a little longer and see what I can do for you."

She was against him for a moment.

"I will enjoy persuading you," she said. "Perhaps even tomorrow."

Their hands rose and fell again. Dilvish glanced toward Reena and Reynar. They seemed to be talking, but he could not overhear what was being said.

As Reena rose from a curtsey in time to the music, she noted the direction of her partner's gaze and smiled.

"Ah, lady! You're about to pop out of that gown," he said. " 'Tis pity we're not alone somewhere, where the matter might be pursued to its proper conclusion."

"For how long have you known Oele?" Reena asked, still smiling.

"A few weeks."

"Men are hardly models of loyalty," she said. "But even so, it seems brief even for an infatuation."

"Well, now . . ." His face grew serious. He looked away from her breasts and glanced at Oele. "I've no reason to lie to a stranger. She's lovely and lively— but I'm just a bit afraid of her. You see, she's a sorceress."

"Nonsense," said Reena. "She did not respond to any of the recognition signs common in the profession when I made them to her."

"You?" he said, his eyes widening. "I don't believe it!"

She gestured and the room vanished. They danced through phosphorescent caverns, towering stalagmites standing like pillars all about. Moments later they swirled across pale sands on a green sea bottom, bright corals and brighter fish at every hand. This, too, passed in an instant, to be replaced by the star-strewn darkness of outer space, far from any habitation of men. Giantlike, godlike, they trod the constellations, silently, to the omnipresent measures of the dance. Her hand passed like a slow, flickering comet before his eyes. They were back in the firelit, candlelit hall again, continuing the dance, and not a step missed.

"I say that your lady is not a sorceress," Reena stated. "I really ought to know."

"Then what is she?" he asked. "I know she's certain powers to command. She's knocked men unconscious with a gesture. She's filled my fists with gold when there was no gold."

"That gold will turn to pebbles and dust," Reena said.

" 'Tis a good thing then that I spent it quickly," he replied. "I'd best avoid certain people next I pass that way. But if that isn't sorcery, what is?"

"Sorcery," she replied, "is an art. It requires considerable study and discipline. One must generally apply oneself for a fairly long period even to obtain the relatively modest status I have achieved. But there are some other routes to magical power. One might be born with a natural aptitude and be able to produce many of the effects without the training. This is mere wizardry, however, and sooner or later—unless one is very lucky or careful—such a one gets into trouble from lack of knowledge concerning the laws involved in the phenomena. I do not believe that this is the case with your lady, though. A wizard usually bears some identifying mark visible to others in the trade."

"What then is her secret?"

"She may draw her power directly from a magical being she either serves or controls."

Reynar's eyes widened and he looked toward Oele again. He licked his lips and nodded.

"I believe that's it," he said. Then: "Tell me, is such power transferable? Can it be shared?"

"Why, yes," she answered. "It could be done. The other would serve, also—or share control, as the case may be."

"Is there any danger in such a thing?"

"Well . . . possibly. There are too many things about the situation that I do not understand. But why would she want to share her power? I wouldn't."

He looked away.

"Perhaps I have too high an opinion of myself," he finally said. "How long will you be about?"

"We should be leaving in the morning."

"Where are you headed?"

"Southward."

"On your mission of vengeance?"

She shook her head.

"Not mine. His. I'll be starting a new life, perhaps in Tooma. He will be continuing on. I don't believe I can talk him out of it—or should if I could."

"In other words, you'll be going your own ways before very long?"

The right corner of her mouth tightened.

"It looks that way."

"Supposing," he said, "supposing we both just

chucked everything and ran away together? I've my own ship, and it's south I'd be going if I were to be leaving suddenly. There are a lot of strange and interesting ports. There would be some excitement, new foods, dancing—and of course the good company of myself."

Reena was surprised to find herself blushing.

"But we've just met," she said. "I hardly know you at all. I—"

"It does work both ways, and I'll admit I'm an impulsive devil. But I've always been good to my women, for so long as we're together."

She laughed.

"It's a little too sudden, but thank you anyway. Besides," she said, "I'm more than a little afraid of the sea."

He shook his head.

"I had to try, as you're the loveliest thing I've ever seen. If you should change your mind while you're still in a position to do something about it, remember that I'm wavering here myself because of my fear. Your decision would make mine."

"I'm flattered," she said, "and it might be fun for a time, but no. You will have to make your own decision, for yourself."

"Then I've a mind to go along with things," he said, "and see what happens. The gain might still be great."

"I might guess at the things," said she, "and I wish you luck. When?"

He looked to the window, where a pale glow was now visible.

"The moon is rising," he replied.

"I'd suspected as much."

"How?"

"From your actions, your feelings."

"Well, is there any advice you might give me, seeing as you're familiar with these matters?"

She stared into his eyes.

"Run away," she said. "Go back to your ship, to the sea. Forget it."

154

"I've come this far," he answered.

She reached out and brushed her fingertips across his forehead as the music moved them nearer.

"Already the mark of death is beginning to appear upon your brow. Do as I say."

He smiled crookedly.

"You're a lovely lady, and mayhap a bit jealous of your skills—or fearful of what may happen should I gain a few myself. As I say, I've come this far, and I've a fair wind at my back. It's more to the setting of the sails I'd be concerned."

"In that case," she replied, "I can only give you a general caution: Be wary of what you may be presented to eat or drink."

"That's all?"

"Yes."

He smiled again.

"After a meal like this, that should be no problem. I'll be remembering you, and we may get together yet."

She blushed again and looked away.

Later, as the music drew to a close, he took her hand and led her back to the table for a sweet and a final round of wine.

When they had finished and were retiring, Dilvish felt a tugging at his sleeve as he followed the others from the hall. Turning, he saw that it was the old man who had sat by the fire.

"Good evening to you," Dilvish said.

"Good evening, sir. Tell me, are you going to be leaving now?"

Dilvish shook his head.

"We will be staying the night, leaving in the morning. Did you wish to travel with us?"

"No, merely to repeat my caution."

"What do you know that I don't?" Dilvish asked.

"I am not a philosopher, to answer such a thing," the man stated, taking hold of his staff, turning and limping off toward the kitchen.

*   *   *

. . . There was Jelerak, leaning above the sacrifice. Dilvish advanced upon him, blade in hand, kicking aside magical paraphernalia, cursing, rushing to the aid of the victim. Only . . . only now he was not rushing. He felt his limbs grow heavy, his movements slow. When he looked into the hate-filled eyes of the shadowy figure hovering before him, he looked past his own clenched fist, unnaturally whitened, grown stonelike in response to the clipped words that had summoned the forces that fell upon him like a torrent, constricting his insides, slowing his heartbeat . . . . He swayed, he halted and grew numb—except for his spinal column, which seemed to be afire. Something was wrenching at his consciousness and a faint, gibbering voice reached him through a sound like a roaring wind. It felt as if he were being torn out of his body. . . .

He was being shaken. He raised his hands and lowered them again. The panic began to recede as he realized that he was in bed.

"It's all right," Reena was saying. "A dream, a bad dream . . . It's all right."

"Yes," Dilvish finally said, rubbing his eyes. "Yes . . ."

He dropped his hands, patted her thigh.

"Thanks," he said. "Sorry to wake you."

"Go back to sleep," she answered.

"What is that?"

"What?"

"To the right," he said softly. "Look at the door."

There was a long pause, then: "I don't see it. . . ."

"Neither do I."

He swung his feet to the floor, rose, and crossed the room. He halted near the place where the doorway should have been. He reached out and touched the wall, pressed upon it. He ran his fingertips along the stone. He moved from one corner to the other.

"It's not just a trick of the darkness," he said. "There is no door."

"Magic?" she said. "Or masonry?"

"I can't tell, and it doesn't matter," he replied. "Either way, we're prisoners. Get up and get dressed. Get your things together."

"Why?"

"Why? I'm going to try to get us out of here."

He moved across the room toward the narrow window.

"Wait! Are you certain it would be wise, even if you can find a way?"

"Yes," he replied. "When someone makes me a prisoner, I am certain that it is better not to remain one."

"But no attempt has been made to harm us—"

"Yet," he said. "I don't understand what you're getting at."

"It might be more dangerous outside than it is in here."

"Why do you say that?"

"Something is going on out there tonight. Something dangerous, I believe, from—hints—I got when I was talking with Reynar. I feel safe here. Why don't we just wait—until morning?"

"I will not be controlled," Dilvish stated, "if there is something I can do about it."

He leaned his head into the narrow window and shouted:

"Black! I need you! We're walled into this room! Come to me!"

There was movement within the well of shadow below and to his right. Moonlight touching its eyes to fire, the dark horse shape advanced several paces and halted. Abruptly it threw back its head and emitted a wailing note that caused Dilvish to draw away from the aperture.

"Black! What is it! What's the matter?" he cried.

"Just burned myself" came the reply. "Someone's encircled me. Can you break it from there?"

"I don't think so. Wait a minute."

He turned toward the bed.

"Someone's bound Black—" he began.

"I heard," she said. "I can't loosen it from here."

157

"All right."

He located his clothing and began dressing.

"What are you going to do?"

"It'll be a bit of a squeeze, but I believe I can get through that window."

"Those are flagstones down there."

He picked up a blanket and knotted it about the nearest bedpost.

"We've enough linen to get me far enough down to drop. Get the basin and soak it all. It's stronger that way. I don't think the bed can be moved, though. . . . No, it won't budge."

He finished knotting the bedclothes together and slung his blade over his back. He raised the damp line and cast it out the window.

"All right. I'm going now," he said, kicking over a stool and mounting it. "Get ready. I'll be back for you shortly."

"But how—"

"Just do it."

He was already edging his way through the window. He had to pause to unsling his blade, holding it in one hand and the line in the other. He stopped, exhaled heavily, and resumed pushing himself to the left, slowly, feeling the stone grate across his backbone. Expelling more breath, he continued to slip sideways, his sternum also scraping slowly past the narrowest portion of the window. A cold night wind fell upon his face as he came free and reslung the blade over his back. Taking the line into both hands, he began his descent.

His Elfboots found purchase where others might have slipped. Leaning heavily, straining his arms, he backed down the wall. He paused to wipe his hands one by one as he descended, his weight wringing moisture from the taut cloth. He looked up once, looked down several times. The moon, climbing toward midheaven, cast a milky film upon the still courtyard beneath him and the grainy wall upon which he trod.

His intention when he reached the end of the line

was to hang suspended at arm's length before dropping the remaining distance. However, his hands slipped free before he could achieve this position. As he tumbled backward, he felt his body jerked about, repositioned with respect to the ground, his charmed boots calling upon the forces necessary to assure his landing upon his feet.

He bent his knees. He threw himself forward into a roll as soon as he struck, his ankles still taking a heavy jolt upon the unyielding surface.

He rose quickly and buckled on his sword belt in a more traditional fashion, looking about, listening the while for any indications of approaching danger. Save for the wind and his own heavy breathing, however, he heard nothing. Nor did he see anything out of the ordinary.

He moved across the courtyard quickly and stood before Black.

"Who did it?" he asked.

"I don't know. I wasn't even aware that I was bound until I attempted to depart. Had I known what was going on, I certainly wouldn't have waited here for them to finish it. I can refresh you on the loosening procedure if you do not recall—"

"It takes too long," said Dilvish. "Since I can do a few things you can't, I'm simply going to break the circle and bring you out."

"It will be painful. It's a strong one."

Dilvish chuckled softly.

"Whatever, I've felt worse."

He moved forward, feeling first a tingling, then a fiery pain as he neared his mount. He paused for a moment in its midst and it rose to an agonizing peak, as if his entire body were burning inside and out, his head swimming. Then it began to subside. He reached out and touched Black with both hands.

"I've drained off the worst of it," he said, and he mounted. "Let's go!"

Black began to move. There was a tingling sensation, and then they were crossing the courtyard, head-

159

ing toward the main entrance. Moments later they were through it.

"Up that stairway!" Dilvish said, and Black sprang forward, hooves clattering. "To the right and around when you reach the top. Then up the next stair."

Large standing candles flickered as they passed, tapestries flapped, hanging weapons chattered against stone walls.

"Turn right here"—at the top of the second stair. "Turn again—right. Slow now . . . Near the middle of the corridor. Hold it!"

Dilvish slid down and approached the wall, placing his hands flat upon it.

"It was here," he said. "Right about here—the door. Reena!"

"Yes"—faintly—from beyond the wall.

"I don't know what they did with it," Dilvish said. "But we need another one."

"I've a feeling," Black said slowly, "that the original one is still there, somewhere—that you were trapped by an illusion. But it is only a feeling, and I can't detect it either now. So we will start from scratch, so to speak."

Black reared, casting a giant shadow. As he did, there followed the first silence since they had entered the building. Through it, beyond it, Dilvish thought that he heard voices and footsteps, coming from the vicinity of the stair. No one was in sight, however, and moments later the nearer silence was shattered as Black's forelegs descended to strike against the wall.

Dilvish drew back as chips of stone flew about the hallway. Already Black was rearing again. His second blow struck sparks from the stone. The third time that he lunged a crack appeared within the wall.

A group of servants entered the corridor, clubs in their hands. They halted as Black rose up and struck again.

The woman, Andra, moved forward, calling to him.

"You said that the metal beast would not move!" she cried.

160

". . . And I meant it—until I was made a prisoner," he answered.

Black crashed against the wall once again. Stone shattered and fell away. A head-sized hole appeared.

After several moments' hesitation, the servants—four men and two women—began to advance. Dilvish drew his blade. Black's next assault upon the wall tripled the size of the opening.

Dilvish moved toward the approaching servants. He lowered the point of his blade and drew it across the floor.

"I'll dismember the first person who crosses that line," he stated.

From behind him there came another crash and the sound of more falling masonry.

The advancing figures hesitated, halted. Black's next blow seemed to cause the entire castle to shudder.

"I'm through," he said simply, backing away from the opening.

"Reena?" Dilvish inquired, not moving his eyes from his muttering adversaries.

"Yes." Her voice was clear and near.

"Mount," he said. "We're getting out of here."

"Yes."

Dilvish heard the movements behind him. Then Black's shadow slid forward. He glanced up, mounted quickly behind Reena.

"Better get out of the way!" he announced. "We're coming through!"

He brandished his blade.

"Take us away," he said to Black, and they began to move forward.

The six figures pressed back against the wall to let them pass. They held their weapons at ready but made no attempt to use them as Black went by. They stared without expression and glanced back along the dust-filled hallway. Dilvish looked back, also, as Black made the first turn toward the stair. The doorway had reappeared, about two feet beyond the new opening in the wall.

Moments later they were moving down the stair. Nothing barred their way. They left the keep to find the courtyard still deserted. Crossing it, they saw that the portcullis was raised.

"Strange . . ." Dilvish remarked, gesturing.

"Perhaps," Reena said, as Black increased his pace and they rushed through. "I have your cloak here. . . ."

"Hang onto it till we're farther away. Black, when you hit yesterday's trail, go left."

"The horses . . ." Reena said. "The other things . . ."

"I'm not about to go back for them."

Black began to climb, beneath a high moon. The cold winds caught at them as they passed, and at a great distance some creature barked, howled, and grew still. Reena looked back once at the castle, shuddered, then rested in the circle of Dilvish's arms.

"You are going to die, you know," she said. "He is going to kill you. You haven't a chance."

"Who?" he said.

"Jelerak. There is no way you will ever be able to destroy someone like that."

"Quite possible," Dilvish said, "but I have to try."

"Why?"

"He has done a lot of harm and he will do more unless someone stops him."

They reached the trail and Black bore them to the left, still mounting.

"There has always been evil in the world and there always will be. Why should you take it upon yourself to purge it?"

"Because I have seen his at closer range than most who live."

"And I am another who has. But I know that there is nothing I can do about it."

"We differ," he replied.

"I do not believe that it is a desire to do the world a good turn that drives you. It is hate and revenge."

"There is that, too."

"Only that, I think."

Dilvish was silent for a time. Then: "You could be

162

right," he said. "I like to think that there is more to
it than that. But I suppose that you could be right."

"It will warp you and ruin you, even if he does not
destroy you. Perhaps it already has."

"I need it for now. It serves me. It gives me an edge.
When its object has been removed, it will go, too."

"In the meantime, it leaves small room for anything
else—like love."

Dilvish straightened slightly.

"I've room for many other feelings, only they must
be subordinated for now."

"If I asked you to stay with me, would you?"

"For a time, I think."

"But only for a time?"

"That is all anyone can really promise."

"Supposing I asked you to take me with you?"

"I'd say no."

"Why? I could be of some help."

"I would not risk you. As I said, I've room for
other feelings."

She rested her head upon his biceps for a moment.

"Here's your cloak," she finally said. "It's cold. We
must be far enough away. . . ."

"Hold it, Black. Stay a minute."

They began to slow.

He had watched Oele dance for Devil with a growing feeling of panic, there before the dark heap of
stones with the silver dagger atop it, cup clutched in
his hand, seeing the bright design occur on the ground
about her, feeling the cold wind.

"Drink it all," she had told him. "It is a part of
the ritual."

Reena's words came back to him as he looked down
into the steaming cup. He had raised it and pretended
to sip as Oele spun away into her dance. He had
sniffed. It looked like mulled wine, but there was a
peculiar odor to it. He had touched the moist rim with
his tongue and known a bitter taste. When Oele was
faced in his direction, he threw back his head and

163

raised the cup as if he were draining it. When Oele faced away, he dashed it over his shoulder into the darkness.

Scheming bitch! he thought. She's not about to give you anything. My lovely Reena was right. I'd wager you're the sacrifice for something she wants. Let's just play at getting sleepy and see what happens next. Bitch!

He placed the cup on the ground and leaned upon the altar, watching the bright design become more elaborate. It was almost hypnotic, the way that she moved. Another man might have bolted and run, having reached the same conclusion as Reynar, but he had been sufficient to every occasion that brought him danger in the course of a very active life. He smiled as he watched Oele's form flowing beneath her light gray garment, remembering to yawn whenever she turned in his direction. Sad . . . He'd liked her more than most.

Then the panic had begun. A chill, out of all proportion with the wind and the night, crept across his neck, his shoulders. It was as if someone were standing right behind him, regarding him intently. He judged that he might be able to snatch up the dagger as he turned and defend himself adequately, keeping the altar between himself and his abrupt companion. Yet . . . He had never before felt himself an object of scrutiny with such intense accompaniments. The mere regard of a stranger had never caused a tingling in the hands, a tightening of the stomach, an absolute certainty of presence. Weakness invaded his limbs as he tried to tear his gaze from Oele's concluding movements to turn and consider the visitor.

You seek to defraud the priestess, came words like drops of blood into his mind, *and by so doing, you would cheat me.*

Who are you? he asked within himself, toward the other.

That you shall never know.

He leaned heavily upon the altar, using all of his strength to turn partway toward the presence, the edge of something absolutely black coming into his field of vision. A force seeming to emanate from it clamped down upon him with even greater firmness then, keeping him from turning any farther. He knew that he could never reach the dagger on the stone—and even if he could, that it would be of small avail against the thing that held him.

He slumped, as if totally drained, his left hand catching at the edge of the stone, his right falling loosely along his side. As he leaned farther forward, he saw that Oele was slowing, that what might be the final steps of the figures were bringing her closer to him. The moon, he had noted, was now almost directly overhead. He still felt the presence beyond the altar, but now its attention seemed nowhere near as intense as it had been moments before. He wondered whether it was communicating with Oele.

As he leaned just a little more, he kept his eyes focused upon her approaching form. Finally she halted, only a few paces away. The dance was finished. He had let his eyelids droop, his breathing deepen. But she was paying him no heed. Her attention appeared to be devoted to something beyond him.

He waited, wondering just how subdued he might really be, afraid to test it. The earlier panic had passed, to be replaced by the controlled tension, the heightened alertness that always came upon him at times of crisis.

Oele seemed to be speaking, though he could not hear the words, and then pausing as if listening, though he could not hear any replies. Finally she moved, passing before him with barely a glance, reaching out, taking up the dagger from the stony surface.

Then she turned toward him, her left hand moving as if to catch hold of his hair.

"Bitch!" he hissed, his right hand drawing the knife from his boot sheath and thrusting it forward and upward as he straightened, even as he felt the chilling power from behind the altar striving to control him once again.

165

The expression upon Oele's face was one of surprise. Her cry was brief and she slumped almost instantly, the sacrificial dagger slipping from her fingers.

He caught her as she fell, turned and cast her body back atop the altar.

"Here's your blood!" he snarled. "Take it and be damned with you!"

He held the knife before him and took a step backward, expecting a supernatural retaliation at any moment. It did not follow. The dark presence remained beyond the form of his bleeding lover and he felt its scrutiny, but it made no effort to control him or to strike at him.

Finding that his strength was with him once more, he took another step backward and began glancing about him, seeking the safest avenue of flight.

"Sailor, sailor" came that voice which now seemed audible across the windy night. "Where are you going?"

"Away from this damned place!" he answered.

"Why did you come?"

He gestured with his blade.

"She'd promised me powers like her own."

"Then why do you flee?"

"She lied."

"But I do not. You can still have them."

"How? Why? What do you mean?"

"Two routes lie before me, and I am more loathe to give up this world than I had realized. I am not entirely pleased by this, but that is the case. Look back upon the castle from which you have come. It is yours if you want it, and everything in it. Or, if you bid me, it will vanish in the next instant, and I will raise you another place of your own desire—or not, as you would. You may have what she had—anything you want that I can give you—for I find myself in need of you."

"In what way?"

"She was my link to this plane of existence. I require a worshipper here in order to focus my energies in this world. She was the last. Now my presence will weaken here until I must retire to the places of the Old Ones. Unless I find a new worshipper."

"Me?"

"Yes. Serve me and I will serve you."

". . . And if I say 'no'?"

There was a pause. Then: "I will not try to stop you. Perhaps I was actually finished with this place a long while ago and cling now only because of certain perceptions it affords me. I will not try to stop you."

Reynar laughed.

"Now, with so many things I'm wanting, I'd be a fool to turn down your offer, wouldn't I? You've just acquired an acolyte, a priest, a devotee—or whatever it takes. What say you grant me whatever powers the homicidal lady possessed and give me some quick instruction in the articles of the faith. There's a little filly I'd be riding before the night is through."

"Then put aside your weapon, sailor, and approach the altar . . ."

Dismounted, Dilvish and Reena were donning warmer clothing when Dilvish saw a figure approaching down the slope of a low hill ahead and to his right.

"Someone coming," he said to Reena, who immediately looked back in the direction of the castle.

"No. From over there," he said, gesturing. "We'd best be moving along."

He finished tying the parcel of their belongings and moved to help Reena to mount.

"Ho! Dilvish!" came a cry from the advancing figure. "Reena!"

They hesitated, staring through the night. Then the moonlight touched the approaching form.

"Wait up a bit! We've something to discuss!"

Black turned his head.

"I don't like this," he said. "Let's go."

Dilvish moved around him.

"I'm not afraid of Reynar," he answered.

For a moment he watched the man striding down the slope.

167

"What is it?" he called then. "What do you want?"

Reynar halted, perhaps twenty paces away.

"Want? Just the girl. Just Reena," he answered. "Unless you want to try being a statue again. We have an understanding."

Dilvish looked back.

"Is that true?" he asked.

"No—yes—no . . ." she answered.

"We seem to have a little confusion on this end," Dilvish called to Reynar. "I don't understand the situation."

"Ask her to tell you what happened to the door," the other said.

Dilvish looked again. Reena looked away.

"Well . . . ?" he said. "I'd like to know."

"It was my doing," she finally stated. "One of my better spells. To everyone else, the door had vanished. I could have walked out through it."

"Why? And how did he know about it?"

"Well . . . I told him that that was what I was going to do. In fact, I had just finished laying the spell when you awoke. That kept me from doing the second one."

"Second one? Of what sort?"

"A sleep spell. To keep you there while I did whatever I decided to do."

"I'm afraid I'm still lost. What were you deciding?"

"To run away with me," Reynar shouted down. "To teach me to use my new powers properly."

"Then I'm in the way," Dilvish said. "Why didn't you just tell me? I have no claim on you. I—"

"I said that I was deciding!" she almost snarled. "It would have been so easy if you had just stayed asleep!"

"Next time I'll know better."

"But I did decide! None of this should even have come up. I don't want to go with him. I want to continue as we were."

Dilvish smiled.

"Then there is no problem. Sorry, Reynar. The lady has made her choice. Let's go, Reena."

"Wait," Reynar said softly. "The decision, you see, is mine."

Dilvish looked to see a bright spark appear in the air high above the hilltop. It raced toward Reynar's extended right hand, growing as it approached. When it arrived, he held a cold blue ball of light that he drew back beyond his shoulder.

"You," he said to Dilvish, "have became extra baggage."

The globe flew from his hand. Dilvish attempted to dodge it, but it curved to follow him. It struck him full upon the breast, rebounded, and hit the ground some eight feet before him and to the left, where it exploded into a brilliant fountain of sparks, leaving a smoking hole in the earth.

Dilvish rushed forward. Reynar raised both hands and began gesturing with them.

Dilvish felt as if he were barely missing being buffeted. It was as if a series of gusts of gale force wind were breaking all about him, passing . . . He continued on up the slope, now able to make out the puzzled expression on the sailor's face.

"Devil lied to me," he said. "You should have been dead by now."

Dilvish's eyes went past him, to the low outline of the altar, Oele's body atop it, small and pale in the moonlight.

"Black!" he cried, as he began to understand. "Destroy that altar up ahead!"

Moments later he heard the sound of metal hooves. Reynar spun, pointing, and a line of flame raced from his extended finger, striking Black upon the left shoulder as he passed them by. The area reddened. But Black continued on his course without slowing, nothing in his movements even indicating an awareness of the effect.

Reynar spun to face Dilvish, stooping to rise with his blade in his hand.

"If the magic won't take you," he said, "here's something better."

Dilvish's own blade, four times the length of the other's, sighed into his hand. He moved forward to engage the other.

Reynar's fingers twitched, and his left hand described a sweeping gesture.

The blade was torn free of Dilvish's grip, spinning high into the air where it passed from sight.

"So it's only your person that is proof against the power," Reynar announced as he lunged.

Dilvish raised his cloak before him, twisting his left arm within it as he did so. The blade tore through the fabric a foot below his forearm. He pushed forward and downward as this occurred, at the same time drawing his own knife with his right hand and thrusting across with it.

Reynar recovered quickly, disengaging his own weapon, as Dilvish's blade struck his shoulder and ground on bone before it withdrew again. Crouching low then, they moved to circle one another. Reynar's left hand made a quick sweeping movement, and again Dilvish felt as if a mighty wind had passed him, though only the trailing corner of his cloak was taken by it. He felt a warmth upon his breast, and something caught at the bottom of his vision.

For an instant he glanced downward. There, where it had come free of his shirt, the charm the old man had given him was glowing faintly. He shook the cloak as Reynar thrust again, baffling the blade and riposting immediately, though he slashed only air, for the sailor had retreated nimbly. In the distance he heard the first crashing blow as Black struck at the altar.

Reynar's eyes had widened the moment they had rested upon the glowing amulet, as if some suspicion had at that instant been born. They were narrowed now, however, as he moved rapidly, almost too rapidly, to Dilvish's left. Dilvish half anticipated the stumble and quick recovery that followed. When that left hand moved again, it was not magic but a handful of dirt that was cast toward his face.

Loathe to lower the cloak, Dilvish shielded his eyes

with his right forearm and twisted to the side, knowing that an attack would follow immediately. Reynar's knife grazed across his ribs on the left side. Hand still high, unable to gain a thrusting position in time, he brought the pommel of his weapon down upon the shoulder he had cut earlier. He heard a sharp intake of breath from the other and attempted to grapple with him. But Reynar pushed him away and danced back, tossing the blade from his right hand to his left, springing forward and slashing with it.

Dilvish felt the cut across the back of his hand as he heard Black strike at the altar stones again. He riposted, but Reynar was already out of range. Both their glances were momentarily drawn by a faint reddish light upon the hilltop, haloing Black and the altar.

Reynar raised his right hand, pointing at Dilvish as he had at Black earlier. The flame leaped toward his breast, struck in the vicinity of the glowing amulet, and veered away as if reflected from a mirror. Reynar immediately followed this with another attack with his blade.

He rushed and came in low. Dilvish struck the blade down. Reynar straightened suddenly then and his right hand shot forward, seizing the charm and jerking hard upon it.

The strand parted and Reynar retreated, bearing it away with him.

Above them the red glow brightened as Black reared once more, very slowly, as if struggling against some opposing force.

"Now let's see how you fare!" Reynar cried, and the fires danced at his fingertips, spread, and coalesced into a sword of flame.

As he stepped forward, the light flickered and died on the hilltop to the accompaniment of a shattering sound. Rocks bounced past them as Dilvish retreated, flapping his cloak, his own blade held low.

Reynar's attack cut a large rent in the material. Dilvish continued to retreat, and as the other bran-

171

dished the blazing weapon it began to fade, flickering once—twice—and was gone.

"The story of my life," Reynar remarked, shaking his head. "The good things always seem to melt away."

"Let's just call the damned thing off," Dilvish said. "Your power is broken."

"Perhaps you're right," Reynar answered, lowering his remaining blade and taking a step forward.

He was standing uphill of Dilvish, and suddenly he dropped, sliding downward, his left foot hooking behind the heel of Dilvish's extended right leg, his right foot striking Dilvish below the kneecap, straightening, pushing.

As Dilvish toppled backward, Reynar was already recovering. He sprang forward as soon as he had, blade upraised, casting himself down toward the other's supine form.

Dilvish shook his head clear as Reynar launched himself, rolled once, and twisted. He blocked with his right arm as he moved his left into position. He felt Reynar stiffen as he struck the ground beside him, impaling himself upon the blade Dilvish had transferred. He held off Reynar's knife hand until the strength went out of it. Then he rose to one knee and turned the man over onto his back.

The sailor's face twisted in the moonlight.

"Leaping and not looking again . . ." he muttered. "It's finally caught up with me. . . . Ow! that smarts! Don't be pulling it out—till after I'm gone, will you?"

Dilvish shook his head.

"—sorry I ever met her!"

Dilvish did not ask to whom he referred.

"I don't know—why he should have given me the power—you the protection . . ."

"I met a man not too long ago," Dilvish replied, "who was possessed of two very different minds in the one body. And I've heard of others. If it can be so with a man, then why not a god?"

"Devil," Reynar stated.

"Perhaps the distinction between the two is not so

172

sharp as men would think—especially when times grow hard. I knew this place long ago. It was different."

"The devil with them all, Dilvish the damned! The devil with them all!"

Something went out of him and Reynar slumped, his face finally loosening.

Dilvish withdrew his blade and cleaned it. Only then did he look up at Black, who had approached noiselessly and stood watching. Reena stood farther away, weeping.

"Your sword fell over there," Black said, turning his head back and to his right. "I passed it on the way down."

"Thanks," said Dilvish, rising.

". . . And the castle is gone. I noticed that on the way down, too."

Dilvish turned and stared.

"I wonder what became of our horses?"

"They are wandering below. I can fetch them."

"Do it, then."

Black turned and moved off.

Dilvish walked over to Reena.

"Can't dig here," he said. "I'll have to use rocks."

Reena nodded. He reached out and squeezed her shoulder.

"You couldn't have foreseen all this."

"I saw more than I realized," she said. "I wish now I'd realized more—or seen less."

She turned away and his hand slipped from her shoulder. He went to fetch the other blade.

They had traveled this night until they came to a rocky bay free of the winds, near to the edge of the snowline, just above the point where the trail began its downward twisting toward the plains and springtime. There they sheltered and slept, the horses roped in at the rear of the windbreak behind them, Black as still as a piece of the landscape farther ahead.

Dilvish stirred from his sleep as the sky grew pink in the east. His wounds throbbing dully, he sat up

173

and drew on his boots. Neither Reena nor Black stirred as he passed, heading toward the skin-clad figure with the staff at the right of the trail.

"Good morning," he said softly.

The old man nodded.

"I want to thank you for the charm. It saved my life."

"I know."

"Why did you do it?"

"You once made an offering to Taksh'mael."

"That is so important?"

"You are the last to remember his name."

"Don't you count?"

"I cannot qualify as a worshipper, save in the most narcissistic sense."

Dilvish looked at him once again. The figure seemed taller, nobler, and there was that in his eyes which caused him to look instantly away—a sense of unearthly depth, a power.

"I am going now," he continued. "It was not easy to free myself from this place. Come, walk with me a way."

He turned and moved upward without looking back. Dilvish followed him toward the fringes of the snow, his breath steaming before him.

"Is it a good place to which you go?"

"I like to think so. I heard you earlier. It is true that anyone can be of—two minds. Now I am of but one, and I owe you thanks for that."

Dilvish blew upon his hands and rubbed them together as the landscape grew white about them.

"At the moment, I am possessed of more power than I need. Is there anything I can give you?"

"Could you give me the life of a sorcerer named Jelerak?"

Ahead, he saw the other's stride falter for a moment. Then: "No" came the reply. "I do know of this one, but what you ask would be no easy thing. It would take more than I have to give. He is not easily dealt with."

"I know. It is said that he is the best."

"Yet there exists at least one who might destroy him on his own terms."

"And who might that be?"

"The one of whom you spoke earlier. Ridley is his name."

"Ridley is dead."

"No. Jelerak defeated him but had not the strength to destroy him. So he imprisoned him beneath the fallen Tower of Ice, whence he planned to return when he regained his strength, there to finish the work."

"That doesn't sound too promising."

"But he cannot do it."

"Why not?"

"Their conflict drew the attention of the greatest sorcerers in the world. For ages have they sought a weapon against Jelerak. When he departed without succeeding in destroying his enemy, they combined their forces to lay a magical barrier about the broken tower, a barrier not even Jelerak can penetrate. Now they have their surety. If he ever presses them too hard, they can threaten to lift it, to release Ridley."

"And Ridley would destroy him the next time?"

"I do not know. But he would have more of a chance than most."

"Could I release Ridley, unaided?"

"I doubt it."

"Could you do it?"

"I fear that I must be going now. Sorry."

He gestured toward the east where the sun was beginning its ascent. Dilvish looked in that direction, to where it parted the clouds like scarlet curtains. When he looked back, the other was far above him, climbing with an amazing speed and agility across the sparkling snowface. Even as Dilvish watched, he rounded a rocky shoulder and passed out of sight.

"Wait!" he cried. "I've more things to ask you!"

Ignoring his assorted pains, Dilvish began to climb, following the other's trail. Before long he noticed that

175

the rough prints grew farther and farther apart, yet paradoxically were shallower and shallower, until, rounding the shoulder, he found only one, very faint.

The following afternoon, they rode out of the mountains. He did not tell Reena about Ridley.

In the high place, when the moon is full, the witchfires rise and the ghost of the girl Oele dances before the shattered altar, though no Devil comes, but sometimes there is the form of another watching from the shadows. When the final stone is fallen, he would bear her off to the sea.

GARDEN
OF BLOOD

EARNING his passage and pay as a scout, Dilvish rode on ahead of the caravan that day, checking the passworthiness of mountain trails and investigating side ways for possible hazards. The sun had reached midday when he descended the far side of the low Kalgani range and moved through the foothills into the widening valley opening into the wood beyond which lay the plains.

"A singularly uneventful passage," Black commented, as they paused upon a hilltop to regard the twisting of the trail toward the distant trees.

"In my day," said Dilvish, "things would probably have been different. This area was full of robber bands.

They followed the sun. They preyed upon travelers. Occasionally they would even join together to raid one of the small towns hereabout."

"Towns?" said his great, dark mount whose skin shimmered like metal. "I have seen no towns."

Dilvish shook his head.

"Who knows what might have happened in two hundred years?" He gestured downward. "I believe there was one right below us. Not large. It was called Tregli. I stayed at its inn on several occasions."

Black looked in that direction.

"Are we going down there?"

Dilvish glanced at the sun.

"It is lunchtime," he observed, "and the winds are strong here. Let's go a little farther. I'll eat down below."

Black leaned forward and began descending the slope, picking up speed as the land leveled, making his way back onto the trail. Dilvish looked about him as they went, as if seeking landmarks.

"What are those flashes of color?" Black asked him. "Some distance ahead."

Dilvish regarded a small area of blue, yellow, white —with an occasional flash of red—that had just come into view around a far-off bend.

"I don't know," he said. "We might take a look."

Several minutes later, they passed the vine-covered remains of a low stone wall. Ahead lay strewn stones in patterns vaguely reminiscent of the outline of a building's foundation. Here and there, as they advanced, they noted depressions at either hand, disposed in such fashion as to indicate that here might have been cellars, now rubble-filled and overgrown.

"Hold," Dilvish said, pointing ahead and to his left to a place where a section of wall still stood. "That is the front of the inn I mentioned. I'm sure of it. I think we are on the main street."

"Really?"

Black began to dig at the turf with one sharp, cloven foot. Moments later a spark flashed as he struck a cobblestone. He widened the hole, to reveal more cobbles adjoining it.

"This does appear to have been a street," he said.

Dilvish dismounted and walked to the crumbling section of wall, passed it, moved about in the area behind it.

After several minutes he returned.

"The old well is still in sight out back," he said. "But its canopy's collapsed and rotted, and it's covered over with vines now."

"Might I suggest you save your thirst for that stream we passed in the hills?"

Dilvish held up a spoon.

". . . And I found this part-buried where the kitchen used to be. I might have eaten with it myself, years ago. Yes, this is the inn."

"Was," Black suggested.

Dilvish's smile vanished and he nodded.

"True."

He tossed the spoon back over his shoulder and mounted.

"So much has changed . . ."

"You liked it here?" Black asked as they moved forward again.

"It was a pleasant stopping place. The people were friendly. I had some good meals."

"What do you think might have happened? Those robbers you mentioned?"

"Seems a good guess," Dilvish replied. "Unless it was some disease."

They moved along the overgrown trail, a rabbit starting before them as they passed toward the far end of the town.

"Where did you want to take your meal?" Black inquired.

"Away from this dead place," Dilvish said. "Perhaps in that field ahead." He drew a deep breath. "It seems to have a pleasant smell to it."

"It's the flowers," Black said. "Full of them. It was

their colors we saw from above. Weren't they there—in the old days?"

Dilvish shook his head.

"No. There was something . . . I don't quite recall what. Sort of a parklike little area out this way."

They passed through a grove of trees, came into the clearing. Large, poppylike blossoms, blue, white, yellow—the occasional red—moved almost as high as Black's shoulder, swaying on hairy, finger-thick stalks. They faced the sun. Their heavy perfumes hung in the air.

"There is a clear, shaded area at the foot of that large tree—to the left," Black observed. "There even seems to be a table you could use."

Dilvish looked in that direction.

"Aha!" he said. "Now I remember. That stone slab isn't a table. Well . . . In a way, it is. It's an altar. The people of Tregli worshiped out here in the open—Manata, goddess of growing things. They left her cakes and honey and such on the altar. Danced here. Sang here, of an evening. I even came to one of the services. They had a priestess . . . I forget her name."

They came up beneath the tree, where Dilvish dismounted.

"The tree has grown and the altar's sunk," he remarked, brushing debris from the stone.

He began to hum as he rummaged in a saddlebag after a meal—a simple, repetitive tune.

"I've never before heard you sing, whistle, or hum," Black commented.

Dilvish yawned.

"I was just trying to recall the tune I heard that evening I was here. I believe that's how it went."

He seated himself with his back against the bole of the tree and began to eat.

"Dilvish, there is something strange about this place . . ."

"It seems strange to me just by virtue of its having changed so," he replied, breaking off a piece of bread.

The wind shifted. The odors of the flowers came to them more strongly.

"That is not what I mean."

Dilvish swallowed and smothered another yawn.

"I don't understand."

"Neither do I."

Black lowered his head and ceased all movement.

Dilvish looked about him and listened for a long while. The only sounds, however, were the rustling of the grasses, the flowers, the leaves in the tree above him, stirred by a passing wind.

"There does not seem to be anything unusual about," he said softly.

Black did not reply.

Dilvish regarded his mount.

"Black?"

Carefully he loosened his blade and gathered his feet beneath him. He moved the balance of his lunch over to the slab.

"Black!"

The creature stood unmoving, unspeaking, like a great, dark statue.

Dilvish rose to his feet, stumbled, leaned back against the tree. His breathing came heavy.

"Is it you, my enemy?" he asked. "Why don't you show yourself?"

There came no reply. He looked out across the field again, breathing the heady perfume of the flowers. His vision began to waver as he stared, smearing the colors, distorting the outlines.

"What is happening?"

He took a step forward, and another, staggering in Black's direction. When he reached him, he threw an arm about his neck and leaned heavily. Suddenly he drew his shirt upward with his left hand and pressed his face into it.

"Is it a narcotic . . . ?" he said, and then he sagged, slipping partway to the ground.

Black still did not move.

* * *

There were cries in the darkness and loud voices shouting orders. Dilvish stood in the shadow of the trees; a giant, heavily built man with a curly beard stood motionless nearby. The two of them peered in the direction of the flickering lights.

"The whole town seems to be burning" came the deep voice of the larger man.

"Yes, and it sounds as if those who follow the sun are butchering the inhabitants."

"We can do no good here. There are too many of them. We would only get ourselves hacked to bits, also."

"True, and I had looked forward to a quiet evening. Let us skirt the place and be on our way."

They drew back farther into the shadows and made their way past the scene of carnage. The screams were fewer now, as the number of dead increased. Many of the men were stacking loot and drinking from bottles taken from the flaming inn. A few still stood in line where the remaining women lay disheveled, eyes wide, garments rent. Across the way, a roof suddenly collapsed, sending a fountain of sparks into the night air.

"If a few should stagger our way, though," the curly haired man remarked as they passed, "let's hang them by their heels and gut them, to square accounts somewhat with the gods."

"Keep your eyes open. You may get lucky."

The other chuckled.

"I never know when you're joking," he said after a time. "Maybe you never are. That can be funny, too—for others."

They moved along a rocky, brush-strewn declivity paralleling the town. At their left, the cries grew fainter. An occasional burst of flame still sent shadows dancing about them.

"I wasn't joking," Dilvish said a little later. "Maybe I've forgotten how."

The other touched his shoulder.

"Up ahead. The clearing . . ." he said.

They halted.

"Yes, I remember. . . ."

"There is something there."

They began to move again, more slowly. A regular flickering of light, as from a number of torches, came from the farther end of the field in the vicinity of a large, heavy-limbed tree.

Drawing nearer, they saw a knot of men at the small stone altar. One of them sat upon it, drinking from a wine bottle. Two others were bringing a blondhaired girl in a green garment across the field, her hands bound behind her back. She spoke, but her words were indistinguishable. She struggled, and they pushed her. She fell, and they drew her to her feet again.

"I recognize that girl," Dilvish said. "It's Sanya, their priestess. But—"

He raised his hands to his head, pressed them to his temples.

"But—what happened? How did I come to be here? It seems that I saw Sanya long, long ago. . . ."

He turned and stared into his companion's face, taking hold of his arm.

"You," he said, "my friend . . . It seems I have known you for ages, yet—Forgive me . . . I cannot recall your name."

The other's brow tightened as his eyes narrowed.

"I—You call me Black," he said suddenly. "Yes—and this is not my customary form! I begin to remember. . . . It was daytime, and this field was full of flowers. I believe that we slept. . . . And the village! It was but a bare remnant—"

He stook his head.

"I do not know what happened—what spell, what power brought us to this place."

"Yet you have powers of your own," Dilvish said. "Can they help us? Can you still use them?"

"I—I don't know. I seem to have forgotten—some things."

"If we die here—in this dream, or whatever it is—do we truly die? Can you divine that?"

"We—It is coming clearer now. . . . The flowers of

182

the field sought our lives. The red ones are those that have slain travelers. They drug you with their perfumes, then twine about you and draw out your life. Yet something has interfered with their attempt on us. This is not a dream. We are witnessing what actually occurred. I do not know whether we can change what has already happened. Yet we must be here for a reason."

"And can we die here?" Dilvish repeated.

"I am sure of it. Even I, if I fall in this place—though I can foresee all sorts of intriguing theological problems."

"Bugger them!" Dilvish said, and he began to move forward, making his way through the shadows around the edge of the clearing, heading toward the far end. "I believe they mean to sacrifice the priestess on the altar of her own goddess."

"Yes," Black said, moving silently behind him. "I don't like them, and we are both armed. What do you say? There's quite a number at the stone and two with the girl. . . . But we should be able to get very close without being seen."

"I agree. Can you use that blade—this being an unfamiliar form and all?"

Black chuckled.

"It is not totally unfamiliar," he replied. "The two on the right will never know how they got to Hell. I suggest that you deal with the one on the end while I'm sending them on their way. Then dispatch that one to the left." He drew a long, double-handed blade soundlessly, holding it with one hand. "They may all be a bit drunk, too," he added. "That should help."

Dilvish drew his blade. They moved nearer.

"Say when," he whispered.

Black raised his weapon.

"Now!"

Black was little more than a blur in the flickering light. Even as Dilvish fell upon his man to slay him, a gory head bounced near his foot, and Black's second victim was already falling.

A great cry went up from the others as Dilvish tore his blade free from the body of the man he had slain and turned to face another. Black's blade descended again, hacking off a man's swordarm at the elbow, and his left foot flew forward, catching the man on the slab in the small of the back. Dilvish thought that he heard his spine snap as the man was hurled to the ground.

But now there were blades in the hands of the remaining men, and from across the field in the direction of the burning town there came a series of cries. From the side of his eye, Dilvish saw a number of figures rushing toward them, weapons in their hands.

He drove his second man several paces backward, beat his guard aside, kicked him in the kneecap, and cut halfway through his neck with a heavy blow.

He turned to cut at another who was coming fast upon him, noting that Black had brained one man against the side of the altar and skewered another with his long blade, raising him up off the ground with the force of his thrust. By now there were cries all around them.

He got inside his opponent's reach and used the guard of his weapon as a knuckle-duster against the man's jaw. He kicked him as he fell and ran the point of his blade into another's guard, severing fingers as he drew it back. The man screamed and dropped his weapon. Ducking a head cut, Dilvish swung low and cut another behind the knee, hamstringing him. He backed away from two more then and circled quickly, getting one into the other's way, beating and thrusting, being parried, parrying himself, thrusting again, slipping around a parry and slashing a wrist. From somewhere he heard Black bellow—a half-human, half-animal sound—followed moments later by a series of different voices screaming.

Dilvish tripped the injured man and stamped on him, caught the other in the stomach with his blade, felt a stinging in his shoulder, saw his own blood, turned to face a new attacker . . .

He dispatched this man in an almost dreamlike series of movements. Another, who was rushing toward him, slipped on a patch of freshly spilled blood and Dilvish finished him before he could rise again.

A club struck him on the side. He doubled for a moment and backed away, swinging wide parries. He saw Black nearby, still felling his attackers with almost reckless swordplay. He was about to call out to him, that they might get back to back for a more complete defense—

A sharp cry rang out and the attackers hesitated. Heads turned in the direction of the altar, and motion was frozen for a moment.

The priestess Sanya lay across the stone, bleeding. A tall, fair-haired man had just withdrawn a blade from her breast. Her lips were still moving, either in curse or prayer, but the words were inaudible. The man's lips were moving, too. Across the field a fresh group of men was advancing from the direction of the town. A red trickle began at the left corner of Sanya's mouth and her head suddenly slumped to the side, eyes still open, unseeing. The blond man raised his head.

"Now bring me those two!" he cried, raising his blade once more and pointing it toward Dilvish and Black.

As he did this, the man's sleeve fell back revealing a series of bluish tattoos along his right forearm. Dilvish had seen such markings before. Various hill-tribe shamans scored themselves in this fashion, each marking representing a victory over some neighbor and adding to the wearer's power. What was such a man doing with this band of ragged cutthroats—obviously their leader? Had his tribe been destroyed? Or—?

Dilvish drew a deep breath.

"Don't bother!" he shouted. "I'm coming!"

He sprang forward.

His blade engaged the other's across the altar, was beaten back. He began to circle. So did the shaman.

"Did your own people drive you away?" Dilvish asked. "For what crimes?"

The man glared for but a moment, then smiled and with a sweeping gesture halted the men who were now rushing to his aid.

"This one is mine," he stated. "You deal with the other."

He moved his left forearm, which was also covered with tattoos, across his body and touched it to his blade.

"You recognize what I am," he said, "and still you challenge me. That is rash."

Flames sprang up along the length of the blade that he held. Dilvish narrowed his eyes against the sudden glare.

The weapon traced confusing lines of fire as the other moved it. Still, Dilvish parried its first thrust, feeling a momentary warmth upon his hand as he did so. From over his shoulder he heard Black's battle cry and a resumed clashing of arms. A man screamed.

Dilvish swung into an attack that was parried by the blazing blade, feeling the increasing heat of that weapon across his wrist as he parried in turn and sought an opening.

They drew away from the altar and the tree, testing one another's defenses upon the open field. From the sounds, somewhere behind him now, Dilvish knew that Black was still holding his own. How long could that continue, though? he wondered. Despite his great strength and speed, there were so many moving against him. . . .

His sleeve began to smoulder as they swaggered blades. The shaman, he realized, was a good swordsman. Unlike his men, he was also cold sober—and he was not as winded as Dilvish.

What was the meaning of all this? he wondered, throwing a head cut that he knew would not get through the other's guard, backing away, and parrying the riposting chest cut that arrived with great force, pretending to stumble and recovering, hopefully to make the other overconfident. Why were they here?

186

Why had Black been transformed, and the two of them set upon the scene of this ancient massacre?

He continued to back away, giving only half-feigned indications of fatigue, studying the other's style, blinking against the glare of that blade, his right hand now feeling as if it had been in a furnace. Why had he rushed to the aid of an already doomed girl, and against such odds?

A vision suddenly crossed his mind, of another night, long ago, of another girl about to be sacrificed by another magician, of the consequences of his act. . . . He smiled as he realized that he had done it again and knew that he would do it yet again if the situation recurred—for this was something he had often wondered over through long days of pain. In that fleeting instant, he saw something of himself—the fear that his trials had broken a thing within him, a thing that he now saw to have remained unchanged.

He tried another head cut. There had been something about the shaman's return on the last one. . . .

Had some kindly disposed deity anticipated his action, seen some incomprehensible use for it in this battle, granted him this small insight into his own character as a death boon? Or—?

Yes! The riposte came too strong again! If he were to back away and flash his blade beneath and around . . .

He began to plan the maneuver as he gave ground and pretended once again to stumble.

He heard Black shout an oath, from somewhere off to his right, and another man screamed. Even if he slew the shaman, Dilvish wondered, how long would the two of them last against the men remaining on the field and the men still on their way from the burning town?

But then—and Dilvish could not be certain that it might not be an effect of the blazing blade upon his watering eyes—the entire prospect before him seemed to ripple and waver for a moment. Everything appeared frozen in that instant—his own parry, the grimace on

187

the shaman's sweat-stained face . . . In that splinter of timelessness, he saw his opportunity.

He threw a head cut.

The other parried, and the flaming arc of the riposte came flashing toward his chest.

He moved back, whipping his blade clockwise and around and up. The point of the flaming blade tore through the sleeve of his jacket above his right biceps as it passed.

Twisting, he caught hold of his burnt right wrist with his left hand, blade straight ahead and pointing at the other's breast. Already off-balance from the movement, he threw himself forward and saw his weapon pierce the shaman as they both fell, feeling for a moment the other's hot blade upon his right thigh.

Then again the wavering, the timeless pulse, prolonged . . .

He pulled himself back, withdrawing his blade. Colors—flame, brown, green, bright red—began to smear about him. The burning blade flickered, dimmed, went out, where it lay upon the ground. Then it, too, was but a dark smudge upon a changing canvas. The sounds of conflict grew still in Black's quarter.

Dilvish got to his feet, his blade at guard, his arm tensed to swing it. But nothing more approached.

From the end of the field, in the direction of the altar where the dead priestess lay, a voice seemed to be speaking—feminine, and a trifle strident. Dilvish looked in that direction and immediately averted his still-watering eyes, for there was only light, brightening from heartbeat to heartbeat.

"I heard my hymn, Deliverer" came the words, "and when I looked, I saw that within you which I might trust. An old wrong cannot be undone, but long have I awaited this cleansing, of those who follow the sun!"

About him, as through a frosted glass, Dilvish saw the standing forms of many of the men who had come to attack them. They wavered and their outlines blurred even as he looked. Yet one of them seemed to have come up, soundlessly, upon his left. . . .

The voice softened:

". . . And to you, who cared for this place—if but for a brief while—my blessing!"

The man seemed so near now, blade upraised, swaying from side to side in slow motion. The other men had all become smears of color in a brightening light—and this one, too, seemed to be changing even as Dilvish swung his blade—

The flower fell.

Dilvish put forth his hand for something to lean upon, found nothing, used his blade as a cane.

He heard a single stamping sound, then silence. About him, the place was filled with the sunlight of an afternoon. Amid the long grasses there were cut and trampled flowers, near and far. Those that yet stood still faced the sun, swaying.

"Black?"

"Yes?"

Dilvish turned his head. Black was shaking his.

"Strange visions . . ." he began.

"But no dream," Black finished, and Dilvish knew by the throbbing of his reddened hand and the blood that still came from numerous cuts that this was true.

"Manata," he said, "I will finish the work, for that which you have shown me."

As they mounted into the foothills, Black remarked, "It was good to fight beside you that way. I wonder whether I might learn that spell."

"It was good to have you there," Dilvish replied, as they headed into their lengthening shadows. "Very good."

"Now you can tell the caravan chiefs that their way is clear."

"Yes. Did you hear it, too?"

Black was silent for a time. Then: "Flowers do not scream," he said.

Below and behind them, the smoke still rose and drifted across the shortening day.

189

DILVISH,
THE DAMNED

DILVISH was three days out of Golgrinn, where he had worked for two weeks on a crew repairing the city's walls, which had been damaged during an unsuccessful siege by an outlaw band. It had been hard, dusty labor, but the workers had been fed well, and he had earned enough coin to fill his purse after nearly doubling the amount of his wages by gaming in the tavern. Now, supplies in his bags, he was headed south on a sunny, late afternoon, moving through hilly, forested country toward the Kannai range. Always toward the Kannais now. He had set his course in that direction over a month before, when the blind poet and seer, Olgric, had told him that he would find there the thing that he sought. At an old castle that some called Timeless . . .

Riding, thinking of this thing, he rounded a bend to see his way barred by a man with a drawn blade.

"Traveler, draw rein!" the man shouted. "I'll have your purse!"

Dilvish glanced quickly to both sides of the trail. The man appeared to be without companions.

"Up yours!" he said then, and he drew his own weapon.

His great dark mount did not slow his pace but bore directly toward the man. When the stranger's gaze fell upon Black's burnished hide, he leaped out of the way, swinging a cut at Dilvish as he passed.

Dilvish parried the stroke but did not return it.

"An amateur. Keep going," he said to Black. "Let him spend his blood on another."

Behind him, the man hurled his weapon to the ground.

"Shit!" he cried. "Why didn't you strike?"

"Hold on, Black," Dilvish said.

Black halted, and Dilvish turned and looked back.

"I beg your pardon. But you've aroused my curiosity," he said. "You *wanted* me to take a swing at you?"

"Any decent traveler would have cut me down!"

Dilvish shook his head.

"I believe you require additional instruction in the principles of armed robbery," he said. "The idea is to enrich yourself at the other's expense without suffering personal injury. If injury is to be incurred, it should be to the other party."

"Up yours," the man said, a crafty gleam coming into his eye. He stooped quickly then and snatched up his blade. He rushed toward Dilvish, waving it on high.

Not yet having sheathed his own weapon, Dilvish merely waited. When the other swung, he beat the blade heavily aside. It flew from the man's hand, landing several paces back along the trail.

Dilvish dismounted quickly and strode to the rear. He set his foot upon the weapon before the other could reach it.

"You did it again! Damn! You did it again!" The man's eyes had grown moist. "Why didn't you hit back?"

Suddenly he rushed forward and tried to impale himself upon Dilvish's blade.

Dilvish moved the point aside and caught hold of the stranger by the shoulder. He held a small man with a dark fringe-beard and dark eyes, a silver ring in his left ear. At closer range he appeared older

191

than he had at first, with a fine meshwork of wrinkles about his eyes.

"If you need a few coins or some bread," Dilvish stated, "I'll give them to you. I don't like to see such desperation—stupid desperation, at that."

"I'm not interested!" the other cried.

Dilvish tightened his grip as the man began to struggle.

"Well, what the hell are you after, then?"

"I wanted you to kill me!"

Dilvish sighed.

"Sorry, but I won't oblige. I'm particular about the people I kill. I don't like to have these things forced upon me."

"Let me go then!"

"I'm not going to keep playing this game. If you're so anxious to die, why don't you do it yourself?"

"I'm a coward when it comes to that. I got ready to several times, but my nerve always failed."

"I've a feeling I should have kept riding," Dilvish said.

Black, who had drawn nearer and was studying the man intently, nodded.

"Yes," he hissed. "Render him unconscious and let us be on our way. There is something strange here. A sense I'd forgotten I have is beginning to operate."

"It talks . . ." the man said softly.

Dilvish raised his fist, then paused.

"It can't hurt to hear his story," he said.

"It was curiosity made you halt," Black told him. "Triumph over it this time. Hit him and leave him to whatever fate he has earned."

But Dilvish hesitated before the morass of moral victory. He shook his head.

"I want to know," he stated.

"Damned primate curiosity," Black said. "What good could the knowledge possibly do you?"

"For that matter, what harm could it do?"

"I could speculate for hours, but I won't."

"It talks," the man repeated.

"Why don't you do the same?" Dilvish said. "Tell me why you are so anxious to die."

"I'm in such bad trouble that it's the only way out."

"I've a feeling it's a long story, too," Black stated.

"Moderately so," the man said.

"In that case, it's dinnertime," Dilvish said, reaching for a saddlebag. He relaxed his grip on the man's shoulder. "Join me?" he asked him.

"I'm not hungry."

"It's better to die on a full stomach, I'd say."

"Perhaps you're right. Call me Fly," he said.

"Odd name."

"I scale walls." He massaged his shoulder. "I get into the damnedest places."

Dilvish sheathed his blade, removed some meat and bread and a wine flask from the bag. Black moved to stand above Fly's fallen weapon.

"Dilvish," Black began, "there is something not right about this place."

Dilvish moved toward a small clearing beside the trail, bearing the food. He glanced at Fly.

"Can you enlighten us on that subject?" he asked. Fly nodded.

"It's right," he said. "They've drawn back. They're puzzled by you and that—" He gestured toward Black. "But I can't avoid them forever."

"What are they?"

Fly shook his head and seated himself on the ground.

"It will make more sense if you let me tell it the way that it happened."

Dilvish cut the food with his dagger, dividing it. He opened the wine.

"Go ahead."

"I steal things," Fly began. "Oh, not like I tried with you. Never at sword's point. I go to a place and find out where valuable things are kept. I figure how to get to them. I leave fast afterward and dispose of the items at a good distance from the places I acquired them. Sometimes I'm commissioned to obtain a particular thing. On other occasions I'm strictly on my own."

"A risky sort of life," Black commented, moving nearer. "I'm surprised it's lasted as long as it has."

Fly shrugged.

"It's a living," he said.

There came a rustling noise in the woods, as of a large body passing through the undergrowth. Fly leaped to his feet and faced in that direction. He stood staring for some time, but the sound was not repeated. He moved off several paces then, reached into a hollow at the end of a fallen tree and withdrew a small brown backpack. "Still here," he said as he pulled it forth. "How I wish it weren't."

He regarded the forest once again, then moved back toward Dilvish and Black, carrying the pack.

"You stole something, and this time they're on your trail," Dilvish suggested.

Fly took a long swallow of the wine.

"That's a part of it," he said.

"And we may be in danger as we sit here," Dilvish said.

"Possibly. But not in any fashion you're likely to guess."

"Come on, Dilvish," Black said. "Let's not be foolish about this. He's not talking about human beings. Are you, Fly?"

Fly took a moment to answer, having stuffed his mouth with meat and bread.

"Well, yes and no," he finally said.

A cloud diminished the sunlight and a wave of chill air passed through the glade.

"They're drawing nearer again," Fly said, "gathering their strength. But I don't think they'll hurt you. It's me that they're after. It's only the others that might give you trouble."

"We have to hear it now," Dilvish said. "What the hell did you steal?"

Fly unfastened his bag and reached into it. Something flashed within his grasp, and then he withdrew and unrolled a long, wide strip of soft brown leather studded with a dazzling array of gemstones. He moved forward, holding it stretched between both hands, displaying it.

"The shadow belt of Cabolus," he said.

Dilvish reached forward and took up one end of it. The glade continued to darken and the stones seemed even brighter by contrast.

"Quite a collection," he said, rubbing the leather between thumb and forefinger and touching the thongs at the ends. There was no buckle. "An old piece. Who is Cabolus and why do you call it a shadow belt?"

"Cabolus is one of those minor gods with a small following which had once been larger," Fly replied. "The center of the faith is a town called Kallusan, to the west of here."

"I've seen it on the map, maybe half a day away."

"More or less. He's sort of an errand boy and intermediary for other gods. Makes sure of good harvests for his worshippers, gives them a hand in battle. That sort of thing. Has a brother he doesn't get along with —Salbacus, who is worshipped in Sulvar, a day's ride to the northeast. Salbacus is a god of the forge. The Sulvarans are miners and metalworkers. They are both descended—"

"I admire your research. But how much of this is necessary?"

"Excuse me. I got carried away. I had to learn of such matters in order to become a convert."

"To Cabolus's way?"

"Yes. It was the easiest way to learn the layout of the main temple in Kallusan."

"And the belt . . . ?"

"On the god's statue in the temple, tied about the waist."

"When did you take it?"

"Yesterday."

"What happened then?"

"Nothing at first. I got out of town fast. You never know with these obscure gods whether it's all a fake to keep the priests in business, or whether there's something to it."

"I take it there's something to this one?"

Fly nodded and took another drink. Dilvish ate another piece of meat. The glade seemed several degrees cooler. Branches rattled as a wind rose.

Then: "Nothing happened for the first few hours," Fly continued. "Possibly the theft wasn't even noticed at first. Or perhaps it was thought some old priest was cleaning the thing. Anyway, I had a bit of a headstart. But it was finally noticed and one of the sleepers came looking and found me—"

"Sleepers?"

"Yes. One of the priests is always in a trance, keeping an eye on the shadow land. They take turns. They do it with drugs at first, but after a time they're supposed to get so that they can enter the place without them. Originally I thought it was just a way of passing their time more pleasantly. But now I know there's more to it than that."

"The shadow land?" Dilvish asked, as a strange depression occurred in the ground across the glade, triangular, with small holes forward along the base. "What do you mean by the shadow land?"

Fly ate faster, chewing and swallowing, stuffing himself.

"Another plane of existence," he managed to say around a mouthful of bread, "adjacent to this, they say. Interpenetrates ours in places. Moves around a bit. It's Cabolus's realm, in a way. Travels through it when he's running errands for the others. Full of nasty presences, though they leave his priests alone—take orders from them even, with some persuasion, they say. The sleepers travel about in it and learn a lot of things; and they can look back on our world from there. Must have found me that way. . . ."

Dilvish watched another print form, in advance of the first one.

"Can things from that plane manifest on this one?" he asked.

196

Fly nodded.

"The old priest Imrigen did it himself. Appeared to me on the trail and told me to bring the belt back."

"And . . . ?"

"I knew they'd kill me if I did, and he said they'd send the shadow beasts after me if I didn't. Either way I'd lose."

"So you decided you'd rather go quickly?"

"Not at first. I thought I might still be able to escape. You see, it was the priests of Salbacus who hired me to get the belt, to give his brother ascendancy. If I could have reached them with it they would have been able to protect me. Once they had it, they would go to war with Kallusan. They have parties headed this way to meet me and then to continue to Kallusan once Salbacus wears the belt. But they're not here yet and the beasts have caught up with me. I know I can't make it now, and they will slay me in some horrible fashion."

"How'd you know they'd found you if they're immaterial things?"

"The possessor of the belt can see onto that plane."

"Then I would suggest you look over there," Dilvish said, pointing to where two more of the peculiar markings had just appeared on the ground, "and tell me whether you see anything special."

Fly spun about. Almost immediately he raised the belt as if it were a shield.

"Back!" he cried. "In the name of Cabolus! I command you!"

Another track formed, approaching.

"What if you just abandoned the belt?" Dilvish asked, taking his blade into his hand. "Threw it away?"

"No good," Fly answered. "It is the possessor of the belt that they've been ordered after as well."

Another track appeared, nearer.

Fly turned back suddenly and stared at Dilvish. He licked his lips, glanced once more in the direction of the tracks.

197

Suddenly he cried out, "Look! I give the belt to this man! I surrender it to him! It's his now!"

He threw the belt at Dilvish and it fell across his shoulder. Immediately it seemed as if he were regarding the world through a twilight haze. And then, in the middle of the glade—

With a clatter, Black's form was interposed between Dilvish and the vision. He heard Fly scream horribly, amid a grinding, crunching noise and the sounds of movement.

Rising, he cast the belt to the ground and peered over Black's shoulder. The man Fly lay upon the ground, his left arm missing. Even as Dilvish watched, the right arm, shoulder, and a portion of the upper chest vanished with another crunching sound; blood darkened the ground to the accompaniment of chewing noises.

"Let's get the hell out of here!" Black said. "That thing is big!"

"You can see it?"

"Dimly, now that I'm functioning at the proper level. Mount!"

Dilvish mounted. As he did, Fly's head, neck, and the rest of his upper chest vanished.

Black wheeled, just as four mounted men with drawn weapons entered the glade to bar their departure.

"For Salbacus!" the foremost shouted, charging toward Dilvish with his blade upraised.

"The belt!" another cried, following him.

The other two riders moved to take flanking positions. Black charged the first rider and Dilvish feinted and cut as they came together, taking the man across the belly. The following rider he caught in the throat with the point of his blade.

Then Black was rearing, metal hooves striking out at the nearest flanker. Dilvish heard both horse and man go down as he turned to parry a blow from the remaining rider. His own attack was parried, and he cut again to be parried again.

"Give me the belt and you may have your life," the man said.

"Don't have it. It's on the ground. Back there," Dilvish answered.

The man turned his head and Dilvish removed it from his shoulders. Black wheeled and reared, blowing fire from his mouth and nostrils. An enormous blossom of flame unfolded before him. There followed a hissing noise that rose to a whistle and broke into a series of pipings that receded then, as if something were retreating into the wood.

When the flames and their afterimages had faded, Dilvish saw that only Fly's right foot remained on the blood-wet ground where he had fallen, that a great number of the triangular tracks were imprinted about it, and that a trail of these tracks now led away among the trees.

Dilvish heard a laugh from below. The man whose belly he had opened sat doubled, grasping his guts. But his eyes were raised and he wore a tight grin.

"Oh, fancy, fancy!" he said. "Breathing fire to drive them off. Slaying the lot of us." He moved his leg then and lowered one hand, groping with it. Something flashed, and he raised the hand. Dilvish saw that he had been sitting upon the belt, that he now gripped it tightly, holding it up before him, face soaked with sweat. "But more of us will come for it! The priests of Salbacus are watching! Run! The beasts will return, will follow you as the day wanes! Take the belt from a dead man's hand if you dare—and gain my curse! We'll still have it! My fellows will feast in Kallusan before long, and put the place to the torch before they've done with it! Run, damn you! Salbacus curse you and take me now!"

The man slumped forward, his arm extended before him.

"Not a bad final speech," Black observed. "It had all of the classical elements—the threat, the curse, the proper bravado, the invocation of the deity—"

"Great," Dilvish acknowledged. "But if you'll save

199

the literary criticism for later, I'd like some practical advice: Did you just drive off an invisible creature of sufficient solidity to devour Fly?"

"Most of him."

"Will it be back?"

"Probably."

"For me or for the belt?"

"For you, yes. I do not believe that its nature would permit it to handle the belt. The belt seems to co-exist here and on the shadow plane, and I believe that its touch would be painful, if not fatal, to the inhabitants of that place. It is a nexus of peculiar energies."

"Then I would be somewhat better off to take the thing with me than to leave it behind. It might afford a bit of protection."

"Yes, there is that. It would also make you the object of a hunt by the Sulvaran troops, however."

"How far would we have to flee to get away from the shadow beasts?"

"I couldn't say. They might be able to pursue you virtually anywhere."

"That doesn't leave me a great deal of choice then."

"I think not."

Dilvish sighed and dismounted.

"All right. We'll take the thing to Kallusan, explain what happened, and deliver it to Cabolus's priests. Hoping they give us an opportunity to explain, that is."

He picked up the shadow belt.

"What the hell," he said, and he drew it about his waist and tied it.

He looked up and swayed. He put forth a hand.

"What's wrong?" Black asked.

The world was filled with a silver light filtered through a misty haze. And it was not featured as it had been previously. He still beheld the glade, the bodies, Black, and the trees at the clearing's edge. Also, however, there were now trees where he remembered no trees—thin, dark ones, one of them grown up between Black and himself. The ground seemed somehow higher, too, in his doubled vision, as if he were sunk knee deep in a gray hillock. The horizon was hidden by mists. There was a dark boulder to his left. Beyond it charcoal forms seemed to be churning in the half-light. He reached for the shadow tree to his right. He felt it, yet his hand passed through it, as if it were splashless, flowing water. And cold.

Black repeated his question.

"I'm seeing double—our world, and I guess that other plane he was talking about," Dilvish replied.

He untied the belt and removed it. Nothing changed.

"It won't go away," he said.

"You're still holding the belt. Stuff it into the saddlebag and get mounted. We'd better be moving."

Dilvish did this. "Still the same," he said.

"Proximity, then," Black replied.

"Is it affecting you, now you're carrying it?"

"It could if I'd let it. I'm blocking that plane, though. I can't afford to run with double vision. But I'll take a look every now and then as we go along."

Black began to move in the direction in which Fly had indicated that Kallusan lay, passing into a trail-less section of the forest.

"Better check your map for Kallusan," he said. "Find us the best route."

Dilvish tore his gaze away from the dizzying scene and withdrew the map from a pocket in the other bag.

"Go right," he said, "until you hit the road we were on beyond the turning. It will be easier if we backtrack for a little distance. It should take us to a clearer piece of countryside."

"All right."

Black turned. Shortly they located the trail. By now it seemed distant and twilit to Dilvish. He found himself ducking away from branches that proved nothing more than breezes upon his face. It grew increasingly difficult to keep the two worlds separate. He tried closing his eyes for a time, but quickly grew nauseated with the vertigo this produced.

"No way you could block the vision for me, is

201

there?" he called out, as they rushed through a seem-ingly solid boulder to the accompaniment of sensations that made it seem as if they passed through a tunnel of ice.

"Sorry," Black answered. "It does not seem to be a transferable skill."

Dilvish cursed and kept low. After a time they came to a branching of the trail they had passed earlier, taking the way that led to their left: well marked, fairly level, and descending gradually. They rode into the setting sun, the light of which served to blur some, though not all, of the unsettling visions that swam past them—the sentient-seeming, menacing trees that swung branches like bony fingers, their touch cold, weak, and disturbing; the gray, spinning things that occasion-ally dove toward them and veered away from sword cuts; tentacled things that slithered after, reaching, but were unable to match Black's pace; the icy wind that seemed more than a wind, filled with rushing black flakes and streamers, bearing a charnel-house odor. As for occasional animallike sounds he heard, Dilvish could not be certain from which version of reality they came.

As the sun moved lower in the west and the shad-ows lengthened, the other world with its undiminished silvery light took ascendancy in the duel for control of his senses. If anything, the shadow world looked brighter, though its mists seemed proportionately thicker now. Dilvish was oppressed by the possibility that the objects of that plane might be gaining in density relative to himself as the day waned in his own world.

Something of elephantine proportions approached from the left in a menacing manner. It moved rapidly for its size but was unable to match Black's pace and soon fell behind and was gone from sight. Dilvish sighed and peered ahead, half-palpable plant tendrils slapping at his trousers and sleeves.

It was as Black slowed to negotiate a turn in the trail that Dilvish felt a sudden weight upon his back, felt claws dig into his shoulders.

Twisting and reaching, he grasped hold of the neck beneath a grotesque beaked head thrusting toward his own. The force of the impact and his own movement caused him to lose his seat. As he fell from Black's back, the shadow world faded about him. The creature, birdlike and about the size of a small dog, let out a shrill, warbling note and flapped membranous wings as they plunged to the ground, but Dilvish gripped it tightly and twisted so that he landed atop it.

It turned beneath him immediately they struck, pulling away, flapping its wings against his head. Jerking its neck free, it leaped back, glancing wildly in all directions. It sprang into the air then and glided off to the right of the trail to vanish among the trees.

"What," Dilvish asked, moving toward Black, "happened?"

"You succeeded in transporting the creature from the shadow plane to our own," Black replied. "You had hold of it when you broke contact with the belt's circuit, and you pulled it right along with you. Congratulations. I've a feeling that doesn't occur too often."

"Let's get out of here before it comes back," Dilvish said, mounting. "The feeling of achievement is more than a little mixed. What's it going to do in our world, anyway?"

"Probably follow you to try again," Black responded. "I'll bet it won't last too long, though. It doesn't know much about your world, and predators will smell its difference right away. Something will do it in, eventually." He moved forward again. "Should be interesting, though," he mused. "if it comes across any chickens."

"How so?" Dilvish inquired.

"I recognize the thing from my own travels on that plane, long ago," Black said. "If one of them does get through and finds some hens, there'll be a few broods of cockatrices before too long. They like to have a go at chickens, and that's normally the result." The trail straightened and Black increased his pace again.

"Fortunately, cockatrices don't last too long on this plane either," he added.

"That's nice to know," Dilvish said, ducking beneath a shadow branch as his vision readjusted to that other plane.

Daylight fled the normal world, its forms now becoming shadowy and insubstantial. The other plane grew even brighter, more solid-seeming. To test it, Dilvish reached out and plucked a long, serrated, dark leaf from a tree that flapped at them as they passed. Immediately the leaf wrapped itself about his hand and its points pierced his skin with the feeling of a multitude of insect bites. He cursed as he tore it loose and cast it away.

"Curiosity again," Black remarked. "Don't torment the plants. They're very sensitive."

Dilvish replied with an obscenity and rubbed his hand.

They rushed on for several hours, at a speed far greater than any horse could maintain. Large, menacing creatures were outrun; smaller, faster ones were avoided or briefly engaged. Dilvish was bitten on the left thigh and right forearm.

"You're lucky they weren't among the poisonous ones," Black had commented.

"Why don't I feel lucky?" Dilvish had replied.

At length they neared a rising of the land in the other world, though their own way remained straight and level. While there had been incongruous dips and descents to their own plane, producing the impression of riding through the air above the shining landscape, this was the first point where it seemed to Dilvish that they were about to run into the side of a hill.

"Slow down, Black! Slow down!" Dilvish called out, just as a human form emerged from a cleft in a boulder to the right to take up a position in the trail before them. "What . . . ?"

"I see him," Black said. "I've been checking. I might mention that the place is not noted for human habitation."

The figure—that of a dark-cloaked old man—gestured with his staff as if bidding them to halt.

"Let's stop and see what he wants," Dilvish said.

Black halted. The man smiled.

"What is it?" Dilvish asked.

The man raised his hand. He was breathing heavily.

"A moment," he said. "I must catch my breath. I've been projecting all over, trying to locate you. Hard work."

"The belt," Dilvish said.

The other nodded.

"The belt," he agreed. "You're taking it in the wrong direction."

"Oh?"

"Yes. You'll have nothing from the Kallusans out of this, not even thanks. They're a barbaric people."

"I see," Dilvish said. "I'll bet you're a priest of Salbacus, out of Sulvar."

"How could I deny it?" the man asked. "Unfortunately, I do not possess the power to transport an object such as the belt from plane to plane and place to place. Therefore, your cooperation is necessary. I want to assure you that you will be well-rewarded for it."

"What, exactly, do you want me to do?"

"From this plane we observed the theft of the belt," he answered. "In anticipation of it, our army was already mobilized. Our officers began moving it in this direction at the time Fly took the belt. It is still on its way, but the Kallusans are already aware of this and have mobilized themselves. They, too, are coming this way, from the west."

"You mean that I'm between two advancing armies?"

"Exactly. Now, we also have a number of advance strike forces and scouting parties out. There is one not even half an hour behind you on this trail. They have with them the temple's statue of Salbacus. It would be simplest if you were to turn around and go back. You could turn the belt over to them, and their officer

205

would give you safe conduct back to Sulvar. You will be a hero there, and well paid. On the other hand, there are also some of our people heading to cut you off—"

"Wait a minute," Dilvish said. "Being a hero and being well paid is always nice, but what about this plane and the beasts, which even now, I see, are drawing near again."

The priest laughed.

"The first priest of Salbacus to get that belt in his hands will lift the curse, never fear. All right?"

Dilvish did not reply.

"What do you think, Black?" he whispered.

"It seems as if it would be cheaper to kill you than to reward you," Black answered. "On the other hand, the Kallusans will be happy to have their property returned, and they'll know you didn't take it in the first place because they know who did."

"True," Dilvish said.

"All right?" the priest repeated.

"I don't think so," Dilvish replied. "It *is* their belt."

The priest shook his head.

"I can't believe that there are people riding about the countryside doing things just because they feel they are right," he said. "It's perverse, that's what it is. That belt has been stolen back and forth so many times that we've lost track of where things started. Don't chase after some ghostly notion of honor, spinning like a windmill and going nowhere. Be reasonable."

"Sorry," Dilvish said. "But that's how it's going to be."

"In that case," the other stated, "the troops will recover it from your remains."

He lowered his staff so that its tip was pointed, spearlike, at Dilvish. Instantly, Black reared, fires dancing in his eye sockets, smoke curling from his nostrils.

At that moment a short, rotund man, wearing a

brown cloak and also carrying a staff, emerged from the cleft in the rock.

"Just a moment, Izim," he said, turning his staff toward the other.

"Damn! Just when my shift is ending!" the priest of Salbacus observed.

"Stranger, keep riding," the newcomer stated. "I am a priest of Cabolus. A force from Kallusan is headed this way, bearing the statue of Cabolus. Once the belt is about his waist, things will be resolved satisfactorily."

The priest of Salbacus swung his staff at the second man, who parried it, struck back, and leaped to one side. Immediately, he pointed the tip of his staff toward the other and an oily flame sprang forth. The one called Izim lowered his and steam gushed from its end, dampening the other's flame. He swung the staff again and the other blocked the blow.

"A question has just occurred to me," Dilvish shouted, "with respect to identification. With these troops and gods moving about the countryside, how does one distinguish a statue of Cabolus from one of Salbacus?"

"Cabolus has his right hand upraised!" cried the short priest, whacking the other upon the shoulder.

"Should you change your mind," Izim called out, tripping the other, "Salbacus has his left hand upraised."

The shorter priest rolled, rose, and punched the other in the stomach.

"Let us ride on," Dilvish said, and Black plunged into the hillside and there was darkness.

Dilvish lost track of time within the claustrophobia that followed. Then, faintly, his own world came into view as if seen through a cloud of smoke. He glanced back over his shoulder and saw that the moon had risen.

"I hope you've at least learned not to strike up conversations with people who try to rob you," Black said.

"Well, you have to admit he had an interesting story."

"I'm sure Jelerak has some fascinating stories, if it comes to that."

Dilvish did not respond. He stared ahead to where a small light had appeared among the trees.

"Campfire?" he finally said.

"I'd guess," Black replied.

"Kallusans or Sulvarans, I wonder?"

"I don't suppose they've posted a notice."

"Slow down. I'd say stealth is in order."

Black complied, his movements growing silent. Dilvish still had a sense of being underground, his normal world a shadowy place about him, as they moved to the side of the trail, departed it, and entered the wood. Black continued to move leftward as well as ahead, continuing a circular course in the general direction of the fire. Dilvish hoped they did not emerge from the shadow hill soon, to confuse him with double images.

It seemed a ghostly wood through which they passed, all night sounds muffled, a dreamlike, faded quality to every tree and stone. The movements of branches following each gust of the barely perceptible wind were gestures of darkness overhead and to his sides. He seemed to hear a fluttering behind him at one point, but he halted, waited, checked, and nothing more could be detected; nothing emerged to challenge them. They continued then across this darkened landscape, until Dilvish could smell the fire and hear the faint sounds of men's voices.

"I'd better go ahead on foot," Dilvish said. "Elf-boots are great for sneaking."

Black halted.

"I'll take my time and follow quietly," he said. "If you need me suddenly, I'll be there fast."

Dilvish dismounted. As he moved away from Black and the belt in the bag, the night lost something of its spectral quality, as if the world were being slowly unwrapped. The smell of mold and damp earth grew stronger. The volume of the night sounds increased. The voices from the camp also seemed louder, the fire brighter.

He moved low among screening trees, dropping to all fours, slowing all of his movements as he neared the edge of the camp. Finally he halted and watched. After a time Black drifted up beside him and became completely immobile.

Over a dozen men stood, reclined, or moved about the campfire, all of them bearing arms and garbed as if for war. A number of horses stood tethered upwind. The ground was well scuffed and in places looked as if it had been turned. Branches were strewn about, perhaps to feed the fire. Beyond the fire and to the left lay a platform litter. Blocked and tied in place atop it was what seemed to be a statue, from what Dilvish could see of it. His view was partly blocked by the two men who stood conversing before it.

"Move, damn it!" Dilvish breathed.

It was several minutes before this occurred, however. When they finally did move, though, Dilvish sighed.

"All right," he whispered to Black. "The right arm is raised. I can return the belt to Cabolus's gang and be out of the game."

He rose, moved back, opened the saddlebag, and withdrew the belt.

"I'll wait here," Black stated, "in reserve."

"Very well," Dilvish said, and he moved forward.

He pushed his way through a screen of branches and stood still. Never a good practice to rush into a military encampment unannounced, he decided. A moment later the man he had taken for an officer turned toward him. Several of the men near the campfire also noted his presence and began to rise, reaching for their weapons. Dilvish raised an empty right hand.

"You have received a message," he asked, "concerning the belt?"

The man he had guessed to be in command stood

209

for a moment and then nodded. He moved forward.

"Yes," he said. "You have it?"

Dilvish raised his left hand and let the belt unroll like a fiery cascade.

"I had it from the man who stole it," he stated. "He's dead now."

He advanced, extending it.

"Take the thing," he said. "I'm glad to be rid of it."

The man smiled.

"Surely," he said. "We have awaited this since our priest's visitation earlier. We—"

Dilvish halted, having felt something soft within a clump of long grasses beneath his feet. He stooped suddenly, seized an object, and raised it.

It was a human hand that he held.

"What is this?" he cried, dropping it, springing to the side, and drawing his blade.

He dug the point of his weapon into a place where the earth had been turned. It was a shallow grave. A sweeping movement exposed a portion of a leg beneath the soil.

The man hurried toward him now, his face twisting, but Dilvish flicked his blade into a guard position. The other halted immediately and raised a hand to stay his men, who had begun moving toward them.

"A patrol of Sulvarans attacked us here earlier," he explained. "We bested them, then gave them a decent burial—which is more than they would have done for us, I'm certain."

"And then you worked to remove all signs of the conflict?"

"Who likes grim reminders about his campsite?"

"Then why cover them where they fell, underfoot? Why not remove them a distance? There is something peculiar here. . . ."

"We were tired," the man said, "from marching all day. Let it be, stranger. Give me the belt now and be free of your charge."

He extended a hand and took a step forward.

"Unless . . ."

The man took another step and Dilvish's blade twitched toward him.

"A moment," Dilvish said. "Another explanation has just occurred to me."

"That being?" the man asked, halting again.

"Supposing you are the Sulvarans? Supposing you had fallen upon this party of Kallusans and slain them all—and then, having the message that I was coming, you cleaned up in a hurry and waited here to claim the belt?"

"That's a lot of supposing," the man said, "and like most wild stories, I know of no way to disprove it."

"Well, as I understand it, whichever side's god wears the belt is the side that tends to win these conflicts." Dilvish moved to his left, turned his body, maintained his guard, and began to back toward the statue. "So I'll just restore the belt to Cabolus and be on my way."

"Hold!" the man cried, drawing his own blade now. "It would be sacrilegious for your unconsecrated hands to perform such an act!"

Dilvish cocked his head at an oddly familiar whistling sound within the woods.

"I've been carrying it around all this time," he said, "so the damage must already have been done—and I don't see anyone here who looks particularly priestly. I'll take my chances."

"No!"

The man sprang forward, his blade swinging. Dilvish parried and cut back. He heard the sound of hoofbeats, and a black, horselike shadow slid from the woods to fall upon the other men who were now rushing at him.

Black crushed several of them with his initial rush, then turned, rearing, to strike out with his hooves—and Dilvish knew that the fires would be building within him.

He dispatched his adversary with a cut to the neck

211

and continued his retreat as three more men fell upon him.

He dropped to one knee and thrust upward, a maneuver against which the nearest was unprepared. The other two men separated, however, and moved to flank him.

Across the clearing he saw Black's flames boil forth, and he heard the cries of those who fell before them.

He feinted at the man to his right and rushed the one to his left, engaging him. As soon as their blades met, however, he realized that he had made a mistake. The man was fast and above-average in skill. There seemed no way to dispatch him quickly or to thrust him back and turn to deal with the other who must even now be preparing to fall upon him. Almost frantically, Dilvish commenced a clockwise circling, hoping to interpose his opponent between him and the second man. His adversary fought against the turning, however, slowing his oblique withdrawal. And from the edge of his vision Dilvish saw that Black was too far away to come to his assistance in time.

He heard the whistling again, and the beating of wings. He recognized his nemesis from the shadow plane, flying toward him from the trees.

Dilvish beat down his opponent's blade, leaped backward, and threw himself into a crouch before the second man, his blade above his head in a guard position.

The gliding shadow had veered toward him as he leaped. Now, at close range, it spread its wings but was unable to brake itself in time. It crashed into the back of the second man, who fell over Dilvish into the path of the first. The fallen man twisted and swung his blade at it. It sprang beneath it, spearing his shoulder and clawing toward his face.

Still crouched, Dilvish swung a hamstringing blow toward the other man, who screamed when it connected. Rising then, he saw an opening for a clean cut and he performed it.

Turning, Dilvish saw that the shadow bird had just

pierced the fallen man's throat with its beak and was rising from the red fountain that occurred there, its dark eyes fixed upon him. It beat hard with its wings and leaped toward him.

His blade flashed and its head flew to the right while the rest of it continued forward, spouting a pale-blue ichor from the stump of its neck. He sidestepped and it passed him by, to continue running erratically when it struck the ground.

Dilvish saw that no new attackers were rushing at him, and Black was still trampling bodies. He sheathed his blade and backtracked then over the ground on which he had fought, seeking the belt, which had been dropped during the conflict. Stooping, he finally retrieved it, near the body of his first attacker.

He dusted it off and turned toward the statue.

"Here it is, Cabolus," he announced, advancing. "I'm returning your belt. I'd appreciate it if you'd call off the beasts of the shadow plane and take away my vision of the place. Sorry my hands aren't cleaner, but they came that way."

He knelt and tied the belt in place about the statue's middle. Immediately he felt a softening of the light in the vicinity, and the rough-carved features before him seemed more natural though less human. He backed away then as a light was born within the eye sockets and about the upraised hand.

"Well done! Oh, well done!" came a voice from behind him.

He whirled to confront the less-than-solid figure of the fat priest he had encountered earlier. The man's left eye was swollen shut and there was a cut on his forehead. He leaned heavily upon his staff.

"Astral combat looks as rough as the regular kind," Dilvish remarked.

"You should see the other priest," his visitor stated. "You've done a fine job, stranger"—and here he gestured about the encampment—"with an excellent blood sacrifice to warm old Cabolus's heart."

"The reason was a bit more temporal than spiritual," Dilvish observed.

"Nevertheless, nevertheless . . ." the priest mused. "It is sure to have found favor. Now that the balance is tipped again we will feast in Sulvar shortly, and there will be executions and burnings and much good loot. You will be honored for your part in this."

"Now you have the belt back, why not just call things off and go home?"

The priest quirked an eyebrow.

"Surely you jest," he said. "They started this. They need a lesson. It's our turn, anyway. They did it to us within my lifetime. And besides, the troops are already in the field. Can't send them home at this point without some action or there'd be trouble. No, that's the long and short of it. Some of them should be arriving here shortly, in fact. You can accompany our band. It will be an honor to go with Cabolus—and you'll come in for a share of the spoils."

Black had drifted to them during this time and he stood listening. Finally: "I wonder whether it found any chickens while it was about?" he asked, regarding the fallen head of the shadow bird.

"Thanks for your kind offer," Dilvish told the image of the priest. "But I've a long journey before me and I don't want to be late. I relinquish my share of the loot." He mounted Black. "Good night, priest."

"In that case, the temple will claim your portion," the priest said, smiling. "Good night then, and the blessing of Cabolus go with you."

Dilvish shuddered, then nodded.

"Let's get the hell out of here," he said to Black, "avoiding all battlefields."

Black turned to face south and moved off into the wood, leaving the glowing statue with the upraised arm and the fading priest with the swollen eye there in the blood-smeared clearing. The headless shadow bird staggered through it once again, then fell, flapping and leaking ichor, near a corpse and the fire. From a distance came the vibrations of an advancing cavalry troop. The moon rode higher now, but the shadows were clear-cut and empty. Black lowered his head and it all spun away from them.

The following afternoon, on another trail twisting its way south through the forest, a young woman rushed from the woods, approaching them.

"Good sir!" she cried to Dilvish. "My lover lies injured just over this hill! We were beset by robbers earlier! Please come and help him!"

"Hold on, Black," Dilvish said.

"Really," Black hissed, almost inaudibly. "It's one of the oldest games in the book. You follow her and a couple of armed men will ambush you. Defeat them and the woman will stab you in the back. There are even ballads about it. Didn't you learn anything yesterday?"

Dilvish looked down into her swollen eyes, regarded the wringing of the lady's hands.

"But she could be telling the truth, you know," he said softly.

"Please, sir! Please! Come quickly!" she cried.

"That first priest had a point, I'd say," Black observed.

Dilvish slapped his metal shoulder with a faint ringing sound.

"Damned if you do, damned if you don't," he said, dismounting.

ABOUT THE AUTHOR

ROGER ZELAZNY was born in Ohio, began writing at age twelve, holds degrees from Western Reserve and Columbia, has been a professional writer since 1962, is married, and lives in New Mexico with his wife Judy, sons Devin and Trent, and daughter Shannon. He is the author of twenty-one novels and four story collections. He is a three-time winner of the Science Fiction Achievement Award ("Hugo"), has received the Science Fiction Writers of America Nebula Award on three occasions, the French Prix Apollo once, and has had one book chosen by the American Library Association as a Best Book for Young Adults. His works have been translated into twelve foreign languages and have been dramatized on stage, screen, and radio.

Roger worked for seven years as a federal civil servant before quitting to write full-time. He is a past secretary-treasurer of the Science Fiction Writers of America. His best-known books are probably *Lord of Light, Doorways in the Sand,* and his five-volume Amber series. He speaks often to campus audiences.